"Peter, you shouldn't have"

Jenny gathered up the bouquet of long-stemmed red roses.

"I didn't," he replied.

She studied the roses, perplexed. "If you didn't send them, who did?"

"Look in the box. There must be a card."

Jenny found it hidden in a nest of green paper. She paled as she glanced at the message: With sympathy on your recent loss.

"They're from the creep who broke in last night," Peter declared, his voice gruff with outrage.

The flowers were the color of blood. Now that she knew whom they were from, they were no longer beautiful. They symbolized an invasion of her privacy, attempts to terrorize her, to threaten Peter. She wouldn't feel safe until she disposed of every last petal. Her breath came in ragged gasps as she dumped the box into the trash compactor.

Peter had called the florist. He put an arm about her and led her to the sofa. "They took the order over the phone."

"But they must have been charged to a credit card!"

Peter nodded. "It was charged to a Visa card, Jenny. *Your* Visa card."

ABOUT THE AUTHOR

When Robin Francis wrote *Button, Button*, Intrigue #147, she became so attached to the hero and heroine that she decided to write some more novels featuring the same amateur sleuths, and the Spaulding & Darien Mystery series was born. In *When She Was Bad*, the fourth and final book, Robin says farewell to Jenny Spaulding and Peter Darien.

Books by Robin Francis

HARLEQUIN INTRIGUE
147—BUTTON, BUTTON*
159—DOUBLE DARE*
171—ALL FALL DOWN*

*A Spaulding & Darien Mystery

HARLEQUIN AMERICAN ROMANCE
253—TAKING A CHANCE
295—THE SHOCKING MS. PILGRIM
301—CHARMED CIRCLE

Don't miss any of our special offers. Write to us at the following address for information on our newest releases.

Harlequin Reader Service
P.O. Box 1397, Buffalo, NY 14240
Canadian address: P.O. Box 603,
Fort Erie, Ont. L2A 5X3

When She Was Bad

Robin Francis

Harlequin Books

TORONTO • NEW YORK • LONDON
AMSTERDAM • PARIS • SYDNEY • HAMBURG
STOCKHOLM • ATHENS • TOKYO • MILAN
MADRID • WARSAW • BUDAPEST • AUCKLAND

Harlequin Intrigue edition published October 1992

ISBN 0-373-22197-5

WHEN SHE WAS BAD

Printed in U.S.A.

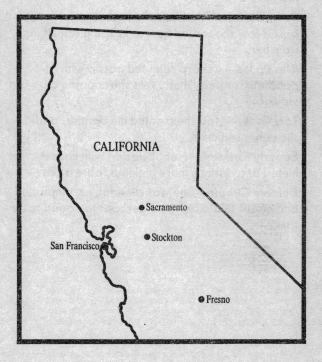

CALIFORNIA

San Francisco

Sacramento

Stockton

Fresno

CAST OF CHARACTERS

Jennifer Spaulding—Was she a victim of circumstance, or had someone marked her for murder?

Peter Darien—For a time, he had restored Jenny's trust. Now she sensed he was keeping something from her.

Rita Eccles—A sharp-tongued gossip with a penchant for petty theft. Was she capable of violence?

Toni Greer—Had she created the danger, or did she only predict it?

Beverly Rudolph—Her obsession with causes hinted at a darker, more ominous, obsession.

Delores Chapin—She was cheerful, accomplished and eager to please—and perhaps too good to be true.

Prologue

She saw him the first time on a Saturday in mid-December. She was on her way out of the Safeway on Fair Oaks Boulevard. He was on his way in.

A passing glance at him left her stunned. He looked so much like Wyatt. Same craggy features. Same rugged build. Same unruly sun-streaked hair.

She turned to watch him enter the market with his long, loping stride.

Even his walk was the same!

He might have been Wyatt's twin. His double. He might have been Wyatt himself.

She felt almost giddy as she stowed her purchases in the trunk of her car.

At yesterday's session, Dr. Everett had warned her about incidents like this. "Sometimes we see what we want to see. It's entirely normal. Part of the grief process, if you will. It's a way of shielding ourselves till we're ready to accept the loss of a loved one, and I won't deny it can be comforting. But if we cling to our false perceptions, if we let them guide our behavior, we must go to greater and greater lengths to preserve the illusion."

"Are you saying I'm delusional?"

Her question caught the analyst in the midst of lighting his pipe. He'd regarded her narrowly, pondering his response, which flowed from his mouth wreathed by smoke. Like the word balloons in a comic strip, she'd thought.

"Not at all," he'd said in his bland, fusty way. "I'm merely suggesting it's time to get on with your life. Dwelling on the past is counterproductive. It won't change anything, and it certainly won't speed your recovery. You need to get out more, meet people, make yourself some friends, and what's most important, stay on your medication. We don't want any relapses, do we?"

"No, we don't," she'd answered quietly, watching billows of smoke rise toward the ceiling and wondering what Dr. Everett would say if he knew that she'd stopped taking her medicine a week ago—and functioned better for it, too.

Under the regimen he'd prescribed, she had sleep-walked from day to day, feeling sluggish and apathetic. Now that the drugs were out of her system, she felt sharper, clearer, more rational than she had for months.

As proof, she resolved to test reality.

She closed the trunk of her car and sat behind the wheel, waiting for Wyatt's double to come out of the market.

Another look at him would tell her if there was anything wrong with her perceptions. If she had imagined the resemblance, she'd admit it. No harm done.

And if she hadn't?

She'd have to think about that. Decide what she ought to do next.

*Five minutes passed. Ten. Fifteen. She began count-
ing the seconds, listening to them tick by inside her
head.*

One, one-thousand . . . two, one-thousand . . .

*She counted to eighty-eight twice, then a third time.
It became increasingly hard to sit still.*

*She switched on the radio and fiddled with the dial
until she chanced upon a sixties' classic by The Doors.*

"Light My Fire." Was it an omen?

*In one of his more poetic moments, Wyatt had com-
pared her to a flame. It was the highest compliment he'd
ever paid her. Flames were more dazzling than jewels.
Less predictable and more elusive. And she had always
been fascinated by fire. Awed by its power to purify or
to destroy.*

*She turned up the volume so that Jim Morrison's
wailing baritone filled the car, and drummed her fingers against her knee, keeping cadence.*

*She was considering going into the Safeway to look
for the man when he emerged from the store, a plastic
grocery bag in either hand.*

*A feeling of recognition swept over her as he dodged
other shoppers and wove through the lanes of parked
cars.*

*She watched him climb into a low-slung black sports
car and knew that she had imagined nothing. Or almost nothing.*

*He appeared to be taller than Wyatt. His hair was
thicker and a shade or two darker. The jut of his chin
was more determined and his bearing more confident,
as if he were accustomed to wielding authority.*

*But these were minor differences. Virtually nonexis-
tent. The resemblance was real! And so was the flesh-
and-blood man.*

She had to know more about him. Simply had *to. She
had to find out his name. Where he lived. Where he
worked. A way to meet him, without calling attention
to herself. Once they were acquainted, it should be easy
to determine whether the resemblance was more than
skin-deep.*

*He was athletic. She could tell that much from the set
of his shoulders, from the way he moved. And there was
a ski rack on the back of the sports car. She noticed a
blue-and-white parking sticker in the rear-window vent
on the driver's side and craned her neck, trying to read
the license plate.*

*All she could make out were the last two digits, but
they were enough to fill her with a terrible elation because the numbers were eight and nine. While the nine
was neutral, eight had always been lucky for her, and
when you added them you got seventeen, a repetition of
eight. A double whammy of good luck.*

When the man started his car, she started hers.

*He backed out of his stall and headed toward the
frontage road that gave access to the boulevard. She
would have followed if a minivan, waiting for a parking space, hadn't blocked her lane.*

"Move it," she muttered. "C'mon, c'mon, c'mon."

*She gunned the engine and beeped the horn, but the
driver of the van paid no attention. She could only sit
there, trapped and raging inside, while the sports car
made a right on the boulevard, blended into the traffic
bound for downtown Sacramento and disappeared.*

*She gripped the steering wheel so tightly, her nails
gouged the skin of her palms. "Dammit! It's not fair."*

*It wasn't fair that Wyatt was dead, while the cretin in
the minivan was alive. It wasn't fair that she had found*

the man in a million who could replace Wyatt, only to lose him again.

She wanted to weep with frustration. She wanted to howl with fury. She wanted to stamp on the gas pedal and plow into the rear of the minivan. But she bit her lip till she tasted blood and kept her composure.

She was on her way home before it occurred to her, if Wyatt's lookalike had shopped at the Safeway once, he might very well shop there again.

Over the next week she drove by the supermarket on the slightest pretext. As many as six or eight times a day. When Saturday rolled around again she spent most of her waking hours in the Safeway parking lot.

Sunday came and went with no sign of the man or his distinctive black sports car, but she did see a car with an identical blue-and-white parking decal, which led her to an office building on L Street, a few blocks from the state capitol.

At seven o'clock Monday morning she pulled into the ramp that served the building and found a parking slot with a clear view of the entrance. Two hours later the sports car appeared, Wyatt's double at the wheel.

Tracking him to his office was child's play after that, and by mid-afternoon she knew his name, his profession and his home address and telephone number.

That evening she followed him along familiar streets, to an apartment complex near the American River—to buildings so well-known to her, they could be considered an integral part of her life.

That was when she realized their fates were intertwined. They were destined to meet and fall in love and spend the rest of their lives together. All of it was pre-ordained.

On Tuesday she told Dr. Everett, "I took your advice about getting back into the social swim."

"Did you, indeed! I'm delighted to hear it."

"Not nearly as delighted as I am." She lowered her eyes with a demure flutter of lashes. "I've met a new man, and he's really quite wonderful—charming, good-looking and terribly attracted to me."

"I'd like to meet him."

"I'd like that, too, but it may take time to arrange an introduction. He's a very busy, very prominent attorney." After a brief hesitation, she met Everett's gaze. "I wonder if you've heard of him?"

"I suppose that's possible. What's his name?"

"Peter," she said. "Peter Darien."

Chapter One

"Tib-fib fractures, slightly displaced." Dr. Clancy slapped the X-rays onto the viewing box and wagged a finger at Jennifer Spaulding. "The season's over for you, m'dear. No more hotdogging till next year."

Jenny didn't look at the X-rays. She didn't have to. She already knew her ankle was broken.

In the midst of her fall, she'd heard the bones snap and felt a jolt of searing white pain. Pain that grew and evolved until it was all-consuming. Pain so sharp, she'd almost passed out. Pain so excruciating, the throbbing ache she felt now seemed manageable by comparison.

I can handle this, she thought, fighting back a wave of nausea. *All I have to do is not move.*

While Peter studied the films, she lay perfectly still, one arm shielding her eyes from the glare of the overhead lights in the emergency room, and tried not to think about the pain. Chalk squealed across the radiograms, and she winced.

"You can see where the bones are out of alignment," said Clancy. "Here . . . and here."

The nausea receded as Peter's hand encompassed hers.

"Tell me, Doctor," he said, "do you treat many fractures like this?"

"She's my third case this weekend. It's a classic skier's injury."

The irony was, Jenny wasn't a skier. This had been her first day on the slopes.

Peter laced his fingers through hers. "What happens next?" he asked Dr. Clancy.

"That depends on whether you want a second opinion."

Jenny lowered her arm, squinted up at the doctor and answered with a shake of her head.

"No? Well, in that case, we'll reduce the fractures, immobilize the leg, apply ice packs and keep it elevated to bring down the swelling. In a day or two, we should be able to cast it—"

"When c'n I go home?" Her mouth felt dry, her tongue thick. She couldn't speak above a whisper.

"Not so fast," said Clancy. "Let's take things a step at a time." He slid the X-rays into their envelope, studying her with new interest. "Did you hit your head when you fell?"

"Dunno," she answered groggily. "Don't think so."

He turned a rheostat on the wall, dimming the ceiling panels, then bent over her and shone a penlight in her eyes. "Where'd you get that contusion on your forehead?"

She raised a self-conscious hand to the bruise. "Brakes went out 'n I had a li'l run-in with a retaining wall. Bumped my head on the windshield."

"You didn't tell me," said Peter. "When did this happen?"

"Night before last."

Clancy's smile conveyed sympathy. "This hasn't been your week, has it, Jennifer?"

"Is there a problem?" Peter demanded, his gaze never straying from Jenny's face.

"Nope. Pupils are active and equal. Reflexes are intact. She's responsive, coherent, able to give an accurate history. Her speech is slurred, but that's probably an effect of the pain medication. Of course, to be on the safe side, I'll order neuro checks—" Dr. Clancy dropped the penlight into the breast pocket of his lab coat and set the rheostat back to bright. "But first things first, Mr. Darien. Let's get her admitted and take care of that ankle."

With that, the doctor gathered up her chart and went off to summon a nurse. Peter gave her hand a reassuring squeeze and left with the admissions clerk to take care of the paperwork. And left alone, Jenny dropped her pretense of bravery.

Retreating behind her forearm, she let the pain rush over her as she drifted into a limbo between sleep and waking.

SHE DREAMED SHE WAS LOST in a snowy wilderness. The ground was white. The sky was white. Rocks and bushes and trees were white, and she knew, if she looked for her shadow, she would discover she had none.

For as far as she could see in that desolate terrain, there was not a single landmark to guide her, nor was there one scintilla of warmth.

She was cold. So cold she couldn't feel her fingers or toes. So cold she couldn't stop shivering. Worst of all, she was completely, utterly alone.

When she tried to call out, the words froze in her throat. When she tried to run, the ground heaved and buckled, knocking her off her feet. When she struggled to rise, an abyss opened beneath her.

And then she was falling....

Falling...

She woke to the predawn shadows of her hospital room; to the variety of discomforts—some large, some small—that had become her constant companions.

For more than forty-eight hours, the parameters of her world had been marked by the white privacy curtains that were drawn about her bed. At the equator of that world, a slinglike contraption held her injured left leg at an unnatural angle that spelled agony for the muscles in her back.

The rest of her wasn't doing much better.

She was exhausted, but she couldn't sleep. There was a wrinkle in the bottom sheet that felt the size of Mount Rose. She wriggled this way and that, but her movements were too limited to smooth out the wrinkle and there was no way she could turn over.

She was chilly, but she couldn't pull up the blanket because she was hampered by the sling.

She was thirsty, but she couldn't pour herself a drink. The carafe of water was out of reach.

She wanted to wash her face, brush her teeth, have a nice hot shower. One of the nurses would help her manage the first two, but she'd have to wait till the fractures were mended to take a shower; according to Dr. Clancy that would take a minimum of six weeks.

Six weeks! It seemed like forever. What a way to begin the new year.

She wanted to go to the bathroom, and at the thought of using the bedpan, almost wept. But she didn't. Crying would leave her eyes red and puffy. It would make her nose run, and the tissues were on the nightstand, next to the water carafe.

Better get used to the inconvenience, she told herself. *The loss of autonomy.*

There was no guarantee the simplest tasks would become less complicated anytime soon, but if she kept her sense of humor, this might turn out to be a learning experience.

The important thing to remember was, she would recover.

In a few hours Dr. Clancy would put on the cast. This afternoon she would be out of the hospital, on her way home to Sacramento. These were things to be grateful for.

Peter was another. She would always be grateful for him.

They'd met a little more than eighteen months ago, shortly after her father's death. At the time, she'd been so devastated, she'd come away from the meeting with only a vague impression of size—of wide shoulders, a rangy build, a deep voice, a broad smile.

Two months later, when she saw him again, she was still engrossed with personal problems, but on that occasion she'd felt a faint yet unmistakable tug of mutual awareness.

A man for all seasons, she'd called him then, referring to his fondness for sports. And it hadn't taken her long to discover how well the description fit.

Two weeks...

That was all they'd had together that fateful June. But they had shared more experiences in those two weeks than most couples share in a lifetime. They had seen each other in every conceivable mood. They had laughed and loved and fought and despaired. They had tracked down her father's killer.

By the time they parted, she felt as if she'd always known Peter, but in those days she lived in Santa Rosa. And although it was less than a two-hour drive to Sacramento, neither of them made it. They hadn't called, hadn't written, hadn't seen each other for more than a year.

And then last summer, out of the blue, Peter had phoned to ask if she'd like some company for the Independence Day weekend. And she'd said, "I'd be delighted to see you. By all means, come on over."

He had arrived in Santa Rosa on the first of July, and turned her world upside down. Before he left on the fifth, he'd asked her to move to Sacramento. She was tempted to say she would, but having survived the disaster of her parents' marriage, she considered love a shaky foundation on which to build a future. Her natural caution made her put off making a decision, until Peter issued an ultimatum.

"Relationships are like people," he'd said. "You can't stand still indefinitely. Not if you want to stay healthy. You reach a point where you have to make a commitment. If you don't, part of you dies."

"And you think we've reached this point?"

"I have. I don't know about you."

She remembered the night in August when she'd found herself literally at a crossroad.

In one direction lay Santa Rosa and the security of the life she'd made for herself over the past three years.

The other direction led to Sacramento, to Peter, to the possibility of love.

There, at the crossroad, on that hot summer night, she had chosen Peter and never looked back.

And on this New Year's morning, confined to her hospital bed, Jenny turned her head to the side, carefully, until she caught a glimpse of the roses Peter had sent.

The flowers looked black in the dusky light, but she knew they were a rich, velvety red. She breathed in, savoring their perfume, and wished she could turn back the clock. Not to the night she'd chosen Peter, but to Thanksgiving morning, to the moment she had decided to take an interest in his hobbies.

She might have shown her good intentions by learning more about baseball and basketball. If she felt obliged to participate, she could have taken up tennis or jogging.

Instead, she'd opted for skiing.

What had she been thinking of? She was afraid of heights, she hated speed and she wasn't athletic.

But she loved Peter Darien, and Peter loved to ski, and when he'd invited her to join him on his winter vacation, it had seemed fitting that she should learn how. So she'd focused on the glamour of the sport. The superficials. The hot chocolate. The hot-buttered rum. The after-ski clothes. And above all else, the romantic evenings she and Peter would spend in front of the fire.

Even though she knew that terrible things could happen to anyone at any time, she had never given a thought to the hazards she'd be facing.

The day before she and Peter left Sacramento, the reclusive creature who managed her apartment complex had warned Jenny that she was in danger.

"There's a threat hanging over you. An aura of danger, thick as a cloud. I cannot see exactly what the peril is, but I feel its power. I know it exists. All I can do is caution you, implore you not to take any unnecessary risks.''

Jenny had listened dubiously and said she would be careful to humor the woman, then put the incident out of her mind.

Shortly after their arrival she had reported for lessons, along with the other beginners. And despite her lack of natural ability, she'd done all right till the final run of the day, when another student swerved in front of her.

She'd tried to avoid a collision, tried to change course, and that was when the binding had given way....

Let this be a lesson to you, Jenny Spaulding.

From now on, she would look before she leaped. If the woman who managed her apartment complex advised her to beware of accidents, she wouldn't be so quick to shrug the warning off.

Danger was lurking all around, ready to pounce when you least expected it.

No one was immune, including her.

BY TEN THAT MORNING, when Peter came by, her mood was considerably brighter.

"It's official," she told him. "I'm being discharged today."

"Fantastic!" he replied with an off-center grin that was gratifyingly enthusiastic. But his kiss was fleeting and light as a butterfly's wing, as if she were made of spun glass. As if his mouth was going through the motions while his mind was someplace else.

Jenny was suddenly aware that her hair needed washing, that her hospital gown did nothing for her. Peter smelled of sunshine and fresh mountain breezes. She smelled of antiseptic.

She gave him a searching glance, and hastily looked away. "I feel awful about spoiling your vacation. Are you sure you wouldn't rather stay on?"

"I thought we'd already settled this." His voice was gruff with impatience and his answer was no answer at all.

Her spirits went into an abrupt decline. "I know we talked about it, but I didn't think your decision was carved in stone. If you've changed your mind—"

"I haven't," he shot back, then, after a brief hesitation, "if I seem preoccupied, it's because I've been worried about you, and—aw, hell, Jenny." He raised one hand, let it fall. "Seeing you hurt and wanting to do something to stop the pain and not being able to, it's just . . . I've never felt so damned helpless."

She met his gaze, conscience-stricken. How could she have been so blind? Why hadn't it occurred to her that he might blame himself for her accident?

"I'm going to be fine, Peter. Good as new. There's really no reason to worry." In that moment, buoyant spirits on the rise again, Jenny honestly believed she had no cause for concern.

At one that afternoon, the sling-contraption was removed from her broken leg and, as she told Dr. Clancy, "I feel as if I've been released from prison."

But if her sense of freedom carried her above Cloud Nine, the weight of the cast the doctor applied brought her crashing back to earth. It encased her left leg, from her knee to the ball of her foot, and left her toes sticking out, pallid and plump as sausages.

Jenny cringed at the sight of them. "I've never been conceited about my toes, but I never realized how fat they are till now."

"They're swollen," said the fierce-looking man who was teaching her to walk on crutches. His name tag identified him as George Burnette, Physical Therapist. The tattoos on his forearms identified him as an ex-marine who loved his mother. "Try nail polish," he advised. "Fools the eye. Makes your toes look skinny."

"Why bother?" said Dr. Clancy. "No one's going to notice her toes. They'll be too busy admiring the cast. It's a work of art, if I do say so myself." He favored Jenny with an inquisitive smile. "What do you think of my handiwork?"

She thought the cast was ugly as sin, but it didn't seem polite to say so. "I had no idea it would be this heavy."

"Plaster's still wet," said George.

Clancy nodded agreement. "Give it time, m'dear. It'll grow on you."

Jenny was not amused by the doctor's remark, but she produced a smile because he seemed so pleased with it.

George finished tinkering with the crutches and backed away, assessing Jenny's stance. "Distribute your weight between the arm pieces. Don't baby 'em. They'll support you. How's that feel? More secure?"

"A little," she lied.

"Good. Then you're ready to rock 'n' roll."

With her right foot planted solidly beneath her, she did feel secure, but she was terrified that when she tried to swing forward the rubber tips on the crutches would skid on the highly polished floor and send her sprawling. She glanced from George to Dr. Clancy, neither of whom seemed the least bit anxious.

Hoping her fears were groundless, she propped the crutches to either side and sagged against the hand grips, white-knuckled.

George gave her a flinty look. "What're you waiting for? Take a hike."

He was not the sort of man one argued with, no matter how apprehensive one was. Shoulders straining, arms trembling, Jenny took a tentative step . . . and a second . . . and a third. . . .

"Those arm pieces aren't there for decoration," George shouted after her. "I want to see you use 'em."

Please, God! Don't let me fall. She stopped to flex her cramped fingers, then braced herself on the arm pieces and redoubled her efforts.

"By George, I think she's got it!" Dr. Clancy crowed.

"Yeah, Doc," said the therapist. "You're a real comedian."

"Better not give up your day job," Jenny muttered beneath her breath.

Each movement jarred her injured ankle, triggering shards of pain. Beads of sweat popped out on her forehead. The muscles in her good leg quivered with exertion. Her heart was pounding as if she'd run a mile, as she negotiated the turn at the end of the corridor.

"Atta girl! You can do it. Only a little farther now."

Drenched in perspiration, she started back, with the doctor cheering her on. When it seemed she couldn't take another step, George pushed a wheelchair her way and held it steady while she sank into it.

"That's enough of a trial run," he said.

He cooled his heels while Dr. Clancy gave her last-minute instructions, then delivered her to the lobby to wait for Peter, who was settling her account.

"This is the end of the line, huh? The last stop on your way out of here."

"Yes, I guess it is."

He parked the wheelchair near the cashier's office, beside a Christmas tree that was dropping its needles and looked as bedraggled as she felt.

"A new cast is like a magnet," he said. "Don't be surprised if everybody and their brother wants to sign it."

She was a little woozy from her last dose of pain medicine, but she recognized a hint when she heard one. "Would you care to be the first?"

"Thought you'd never ask." He fished a fistful of felt-tip markers from the pocket of his lab coat and extended his hand to her. "What's your preference? Basic black or something more colorful?"

She chose turquoise to match her parka, and watched him draw a miniature daisy on the plaster, which he labeled Medal of Valor.

"Don't think I award these to all my patients. All most of them get is a Good Conduct." He signed his name with a flourish, and she summoned a shaky smile.

"Thank you," she said. "You've been very kind."

"Hey, don't mention it," he replied. "I'll just round up a nurse to take you to your car, so you can be on your way." He clipped the pens inside his pocket and left her with a pat on the shoulder and a solemn, "You did good, kid."

And that hard-won praise did more for her morale than all of Dr. Clancy's cheers.

Chapter Two

Peter had done what he could to make the drive home as easy as possible. He'd rolled back the passenger seat so that it was half reclining and used pillows to make a footstool, but there wasn't enough room in the Maserati sports coupe for Jenny to keep her leg properly elevated.

She could feel her ankle swelling inside the cast. She could see her toes expand. She watched them grow as shiny as inflated balloons, so taut she could scarcely wiggle them.

She fidgeted about, hoping to find a comfortable position. She tried everything she could think of—yoga, deep breathing, relaxation techniques. With every mile they traveled the torment grew, and the worst of it was, to spare Peter's feelings, she couldn't let on how miserable she felt.

They had been on the road half an hour when she noticed the itch. It began in her heel and migrated up her shin to a spot below her left knee where it settled, just out of reach, foiling her attempts to scratch it.

She could live with the pain, but this was intolerable. It was maddening. Frustrating. Slow torture. Like having to sneeze and not being able to.

But Peter, bless him, had foreseen this development. "Look in the glove box. There's a little something in there that might help."

The "little something" was a metal wand with a retractable brush on one end.

"Compliments of the hospital gift shop," he told her.

Thin enough to fit inside the cast, flexible enough to adjust to the contours of her leg, long enough to slide all the way to her foot, the wand let her scratch to her heart's content, and made the rest of the trip bearable.

When they reached the outskirts of Sacramento Peter asked, "What'll it be? Your place or mine?"

"Mine," Jenny answered without hesitation.

Her place and Peter's were in the same part of town. Both offered views of the American River, but that was as far as the similarities went.

Peter's condo occupied half the third floor of a glass-and-steel high-rise. The interior featured stark white walls, clean lines, furniture arranged with the precision of a geometric equation—and about as much warmth. The only hint that Peter was not a fanatical technocrat was the collection of neon cacti that graced one wall in the living room.

The cacti aside, Jennifer considered the condo sterile. Impersonal. The first time she'd seen it, she'd been struck by the absence of clutter. Where was the basketball? she'd wondered. Where were the baseball bat and fielder's glove? Where was any evidence of Peter's fondness for team sports?

In the eighteen months since then Peter had redecorated, but her reaction hadn't changed. Perhaps it was the excessive neatness or the white-on-white elegance of the decor, but there was something about the condo that made her want to walk on tiptoe and speak in whispers. She would never feel completely at ease there.

Unlike Peter, who accepted change—even embraced it—as an everyday part of life in the nineties, she tended to resist change. She found it frightening. And if she couldn't imagine him living in a world without Lycra, she couldn't imagine herself living in a world without maple and chintz and Grandma Moses.

Naturally enough, her apartment reflected her own more traditional tastes.

Last September, when she moved to Sacramento, she'd signed a lease in a cluster of eightplexes built Mediterranean-style around a flower-filled courtyard. Peter laughingly called the apartment complex "My adobe hacienda," but even he had to admit it had mellowed into gracious old age.

Thick stucco walls gave it character. Terra-cotta-tiled roofs gave it charm. Balconies with wrought-iron handrails gave it quaintness. Lush hedges and a grove of Oriental plane trees screened it from the street, and the latest electronic surveillance equipment provided security.

There was one drawback, but in her eagerness to get home, Jenny never gave it a thought until she hobbled into the vestibule of her building and confronted the stairs. After everything else she'd been through today, there was no way she could climb them. She sank her teeth into her lower lip, suppressing a cry of dismay.

Peter came to a stop beside her. "Sure you won't reconsider?"

"Guess I'll have to. At least, for a few days, till I'm more adept with crutches."

He gave her a probing look and saw her disappointment. "If you'd rather stay here, I can carry you upstairs, but my place has the elevators. You'd be free to come and go as you please, and in case of fire, you'd be a whole lot safer."

"You're right," she allowed. His argument made perfect sense, except... Her expression brightened. She lifted her chin. "If there happened to be a fire at your place, chances are the elevators would shut down. If they did, I'd have to worry about making it down two flights of stairs instead of just one."

"Point taken," said Peter, hiding a grin. Despite his concern for Jenny's safety, he was relieved to see that the broken ankle hadn't broken her spirit. He mounted the stairs, taking them two at a time. At the second-floor landing, he called, "Don't go 'way. I'll unlock your apartment and be back for you in a jiffy."

THAT NIGHT, for the first time since the accident, Jenny slept well, while Peter played tug-of-war for the blanket, which he needed and Jenny did not.

"It's too hot with this cast on," she mumbled before she dozed off. "All I want is the sheet."

Hours later, while she slept like a baby, he remained wide-awake, alternately shivering and dodging the cast. "Damn thing's a lethal weapon," he muttered.

Now and again he pulled up the covers, but after a scant few minutes Jenny kicked them off, and when he tried to snuggle close to her for warmth, he inevitably barked his shins.

The following morning found her bright and perky— and apologetic for the bruises she'd left.

The apartment manager phoned to welcome her home while Peter was in the shower. Jenny informed her the danger she'd predicted had passed. She described the circumstances of her fall, and a long silence ensued.

"Forgive me," the manager said at last, "but the threat I saw had no connection with skiing."

"Well, then, it must've been the trouble with my car. I had a minor accident the night before we left."

"There is nothing minor about the danger you're in," the woman declared. "It comes from a stranger, that's all I can tell you."

On that disquieting note, the line went dead.

Jenny was ensconced on the sofa, finishing breakfast and wondering whether she should mention the manager's prophecy to Peter, when Peter announced he had some errands to run.

"Your bed's not big enough for both of us, pardner. I'm going to look for something king-size."

"Good idea," she replied, buttering a piece of toast.

"If there's anything you'd like me to take care of, now's the time to place your order."

Jenny wondered why Peter hadn't invited her to go with him. Not that she would have accepted, but shouldn't he at least ask? "We'll need a few things from the grocery store."

He grabbed the pencil and message pad from the telephone stand, and dropped them on her breakfast tray. "Make a list. I'll pick them up."

She toyed with the pencil, and watched him stride into the bedroom and riffle through his suitcase. "Where else will you be going?"

"The office. I want to let Max know we're back."

She nodded. Max Darien was Peter's uncle, as well as his partner in the law firm. "If you see Max, give him my best."

"When he finds out what's happened, he'll want to see you." Peter poked his head around the bedroom door and raised a quizzical brow. "Do you feel up to having visitors?"

"They'd be welcome, as long as they don't expect me to run foot races." She glanced at her injured leg, her naked toes. "Would you get me some nail polish?"

"Sure. Any particular color?"

She wiggled her toes, considering this, and opted for camouflage rather than fashion. "Just something bright. And pretty."

Peter sauntered back to the living room, a crewneck sweater in one hand. "I think I'll stop by my place, too. If I'm going to be staying here awhile, it'd be nice to have something to wear besides ski clothes." He pulled on the sweater and grimaced. "After that I want to see about having my mail forwarded."

"While you're at the post office, would you ask them to cancel the hold on my mail?"

"Will do." Shoving his fingers through his hair, he returned to the bedroom and began cramming his belongings back in the suitcase. "Anything else?"

She ate the last bite of toast, and reached for the notepad. "That's all I can think of."

"Well, if anything comes to mind, give me a call on my car phone."

A few minutes later, her shopping list was completed, and Peter's luggage was stacked in the entryway, ready to load in his car. She was surprised to see him adding her skis to the pile.

"Where are you going with those?" she inquired.

"To the store where you bought 'em. I want to show that guy who installed the bindings what a sloppy job he did."

Jenny didn't see what purpose this would serve. What was done was done. Her ankle was broken, and lodging complaints wouldn't mend it any quicker.

Besides, the bindings had seemed perfectly fine last Friday, when she'd picked up the skis. Granted, she was no expert, but Peter was, and he hadn't spotted any defects till after her fall. And now that the worst was over, she wanted to put the ordeal behind her. *All* of it. The accident. The trauma. The sleepless nights. Her experiences at the hospital.

The last thing she wanted was to get dragged into the process of assigning blame.

But Peter, evidently, wasn't ready to let bygones be bygones. Whether because he was a lawyer, or because he felt partially responsible for her injury, Jenny couldn't say. But he was spoiling for a fight. The way he swung the skis off his shoulder, as if he'd like to throttle them, made that clear. And the set of his jaw told her she would be well-advised to keep her opinions to herself.

She tore the list off the message pad and held it out to him. "Don't forget this."

He loosened his choke hold on the skis to fold the list into his wallet, then sat on his heels in front of her. "Is there anything you'd like before I leave?"

"How 'bout a kiss?"

That brought her a grin and a peck on the cheek.

When he would have straightened, she wrapped her arms about his neck and drew him closer.

"I could use a hug, too."

This brought her a chuckle and a more satisfying kiss.

She brushed a piece of lint off his sweater and framed his face between her palms. "Where's your comb?"

He chuckled again and fished a comb from his hip pocket, which she used to tame some of the tangles in his hair.

"Peter," she said quietly, "I've never seen you so distracted. Why don't you tell me what's wrong."

"There's nothing to tell—only I don't like leaving you alone."

Jenny smiled as she ran the comb through his hair. "This may come as a shock to you, but I'm capable of entertaining myself."

"That's what worries me. That you'll overdo while I'm gone."

"Me overdo? Don't be silly." She wrinkled her nose at him, gave him his comb. "I'll rotate my tires, discover a cure for baldness—"

Peter frowned and pushed to his feet. "That settles it. I'm not going anywhere till you give me your word you'll take it easy."

Jenny threw up her hands in mock surrender. "I promise."

This was an easy promise to make, even easier to keep. If Peter had suspected how easy, he might have postponed his errands.

The drive home, the effort of getting around on crutches, her attempts to compensate for the weight of the cast had taken their toll. Yesterday's discomforts had been limited to her leg; today's were spread from head to toe.

From planning to completion, it took the better part of an hour to shampoo her hair. When she was through it took another twenty minutes for her eyes to stop tearing from the suds she'd gotten in them. By the time her hair was dry, she was content to lie on the couch and write a letter to her mother.

She already knew about the accident, thanks to Peter. He'd phoned the evening Jenny was admitted to the hospital, and he'd kept Phyllis posted with daily bulletins via long-distance. But, as he'd informed Jenny, "Your mother's not going to believe you're okay till she hears it from you."

Hence the letter.

Jenny tried to keep it short and breezy, and she hoped, reassuring. If Phyllis wasn't reassured, she would phone, and if she phoned, chances were they'd wind up bickering, which wouldn't do either of them any good.

When the letter was finished, Jenny called the office of the orthopedist Dr. Clancy had recommended. The receptionist quizzed her about personal data and insurance, then transferred her to the nurse, who informed her she needn't come in until the end of the month unless she developed unusual symptoms.

"Would you define 'unusual?'" Jenny asked.

"Any signs of infection. Fever, pain, swelling."

"What about muscle cramps? A charley horse? Generalized aches and pains?"

"I'm afraid you'll have to live with those," said the nurse. "They're par for the course at this stage."

Thanks for the encouragement, Jenny thought. She had barely hung up when someone knocked at the front door.

She dragged herself off the couch and fumbled with the crutches. "Just a minute," she called as she made her way across the living room, then, realizing how slow her progress was, revised her estimate. "Make that two."

At the corner of the entryway, she saw that the dead bolt was unlocked and called, "Come in."

The door opened, revealing a diminutive redhead whose explosive mane of copper-wire curls made her seem top-heavy. "Trusting soul, aren't you," she observed, peering at Jenny with lashless dark eyes, as if she were searching for character flaws.

"No, not really. But I'm working on it," Jenny said.

"If you're suspicious, you're not alone. Lots of women are these days."

"The crime rate being what it is, can you blame them?"

"Good question," said the redhead, but she didn't answer it. Instead, she offered a ghost of a smile and changed the subject. "Before this discussion gets any deeper, let me get to the point of my visit and introduce myself. I'm Rita Eccles, your neighbor from downstairs."

"The one who plays the piano?"

"No, that's Bev Rudolph, my roommate. Has the music disturbed you?"

"Not at all. I think she plays beautifully." Jenny gestured her visitor toward the living room, with a choppy movement of a crutch. "It's nice to meet you. I've been meaning to stop by and say hello ever since I moved in last summer, but I was out of town for six weeks, and when I got back one thing led to another—"

"Don't apologize. I'm sure you had the best of intentions."

Jenny leaned against the wall, catching her breath. "Have you lived here long?"

"Long enough that I can tell you most of the tenants aren't worth meeting, although you might want to give their monthly get-togethers a try. The food's good and there's plenty of free booze. But after you've gone to one, they're a waste of time, unless you enjoy hanging out with assorted flakes. As for the apartment manager, Toni Greer, take my advice and go out of your way to avoid her. She trades on sympathy. All that black she wears. The crocodile tears—''

"You don't think they're genuine?"

"About as genuine as a three-dollar bill. They're effective, though. I'll give her that. She's a lousy superintendent. The drain in my bathtub's been on the fritz since last July. I think she put a hex on it. But I'm the only one who's filed a formal complaint. The other tenants make excuses for her, and her repair budget's so minuscule, she's got the management company eating out of the palm of her hand—little white gloves and all."

Rita twirled her forefinger against her temple. "Toni's crazy like a fox. She knows all the angles, and plays 'em for all they're worth. That hokum about being a widow, for instance. The woman's made a career out of mourning her late husband, but five'll get you ten she's never been married."

Jenny pushed away from the wall, resolving to take whatever tales this neighbor told her with a grain of salt. "Why would she lie about a thing like that?"

"Who said she's lying? Could be she believes it." Rita perched on the arm of the love seat and cocked her head to one side, appraising Jenny's progress. "You really ought to get off that leg."

"You read my mind," said Jenny, surprised by her visitor's switch from vitriol to good humor.

While the redhead glanced around as if she were pricing the furniture, Jenny regained the couch, sank into the upholstery, put her feet up and heaved a sigh.

Rita sighed, too, and resumed her assessment of Jenny. "So you're J. Spaulding," she mused. "Boy, will Bev be ticked off when she hears you're a female. When we saw your card on the mailbox, we made a bet about your first name. Romantic that she is, Bev figured you'd be an eligible male, so she went with John. I, on the other hand, put my money on Joanne, dyed-in-the-wool realist that I am."

Dyed-in-the-wool gossip's more like it. "Looks like you both lose. My name's Jennifer. Jenny to my friends."

Rita shuffled through the magazines on the coffee table, the image of nonchalance. "Speaking of friends, who's the guy I saw leaving your apartment this morning?"

"That'd be Peter."

"He's awfully good-looking." The candy dish caught Rita's attention. She tested the chocolates till she found one to her liking. "I don't suppose he's your brother?"

"No, he isn't."

"Ah, well. Some people get all the breaks. No pun intended."

Jenny held her breath for a ten count. Neighbor or not, she'd had about all she could take of this sharp-tongued busybody, with her gimlet-eyed gaze and pointed remarks. The problem was, how to get rid of her. Sighing again, wearily, she watched the redhead plunder the candy dish.

"So tell me," she inquired between nibbles, "what do you do when you're not taking trips or convalescing?"

"I'm a writer."

Rita's jaw froze, mid-chew. She raised a skeptical brow. "You're kidding! What do you write?"

"Biographies."

The eyebrow inched higher. "Have you actually been published?"

"Several times."

A mote of respect brightened Rita's eyes. "Color me green with envy. It must be neat to be your own boss, set your own hours. Only what happens if you're tempted to goof off?"

"Occasionally I give in to it, but more often than not I work anyway. You can't make it as a writer without a certain amount of self-discipline."

"But it's worth it, right? I mean money-wise?"

"It's a living."

"What've you written? Anything I'd recognize?"

"Perhaps, if you read bestsellers." The moment the words were out, Jenny regretted them. Sarcasm wouldn't resolve anything. She cleared her throat, and tried a more direct approach. "One of the disadvantages of writing is that total strangers feel free to ask for your credentials. If you meet someone who says he's a Realtor, you don't expect him to prove it. You might ask what sort of property he sells, but you wouldn't dream of asking if he's closed any deals."

"I wouldn't be too sure about that," Rita answered, grinning. "But never fear, Jennifer. I may not be loaded with couth, but I'm not dense either. I don't need a building to fall on me to understand what you're driving at."

"Good! Then why don't we talk about you for a change. What do you do when you're not playing Welcome Wagon?"

"Nothing as glamorous as writing, I'm afraid."

"Only people who aren't writers think writing is glamorous. Mostly, it's plain hard work."

"So's my job," said Rita. "In spades."

"Now I'm really curious," said Jenny. "What is it you do?"

"I'm a nurse on the psych ward at County General. And believe me, I could tell you things about that place that'd curl your hair. Or if you're squeamish, I'll tell you about my roommate."

"If those are my choices, I'd rather hear about your roommate."

"Okay." Rita paused to sample a caramel-pecan candy. "Aside from our work—Bev's a nurse, too—we don't have much in common. When I'm off-duty, I like to go out, have a few laughs, forget about the hospital. But Bev takes life too seriously to see the funny side of anything. There are times when I'd swear she has no sense of humor. She's intense. Too intense, if you ask me. And she spreads herself too thin. If she's not marching in a demonstration, protesting date rape or nuclear proliferation, she's boycotting lettuce or table grapes, or trying to save the whales, battered women, the environment, the whole damn world!"

"Sounds as if she's deeply committed to her causes. Maybe she enjoys volunteer work more than you realize?"

Rita shook her head. "I'll tell you what she enjoys. Sacrifice. And suffering. Boy, does she get a charge out of that! She's the kind of reformer who takes injustice so much to heart, you give your sympathy to her instead of the poor slobs she's trying to help. And what's sad is, Bev can't see it. She's convinced she's making this huge contribution, and if she thinks something's true, then by golly it must be. God knows, there's nothing I can say that'll change her mind."

"But you've tried reasoning with her?"

"Sure have. I don't know how many times I've told her she ought to chill out."

"And what does she say to that?" Jenny asked.

"That somebody has to give a damn. Somebody has to care." Rita contemplated the ruins in the candy dish as if she were reading tea leaves. "Bev's like these chocolates. You never know what's buried beneath the surface till you dig through the outer shell."

"That's an interesting simile. It implies she can't take the heat, that she's firm on the outside, soft on the inside."

"Either that or she's a whole lot tougher than she lets on. Bev's the only one who knows for sure."

"And you're just the opposite," said Jenny.

"Damn straight." Rita pushed back the cuffs of her sweater. "You won't find any tricks up my sleeves. No games. No guilty secrets. No axes to grind. Life's too short to worry about pretenses, so I believe in being upfront. With me, what you see is what you get."

Chapter Three

The noon hour came and went, but Rita didn't. At one o'clock, professing an interest in Jenny's welfare, she retired to the kitchen to prepare soup and sandwiches. "Can't afford to skip meals while you're recuperating," she said.

After they polished off the sandwiches, Rita offered to wash the dishes and when that chore was done, she said she was missing "General Hospital."

"My TV's on the blink. Mind if I watch it here?"

"Well, I do have some letters to write."

"Go on and write 'em. Won't bother me. I'll take 'em down to the mailbox for you later."

Rita had taken possession of the television remote, and the soap opera's theme drowned out Jenny's protest.

When the show was over, Rita signed Jenny's cast. She ate the last of the chocolates and depleted her fund of small talk. She ran out of gossip and wore out her welcome. And still she stayed . . . until mid-afternoon, when she had to get ready for work. Even then, she left with visible reluctance. She also left with Jenny's pen.

"She probably took it so she'd have an excuse to come back," Jenny told Peter that evening.

"She doesn't sound as if she'd need an excuse."

"She has a lot of brass, all right, but she's dying to meet you. I think that's why she stayed so long. She was waiting for you to get back."

But Peter hadn't returned for another two hours.

By then it was almost five-thirty, a wintry darkness had fallen, and Jenny was wondering what could be taking him so long. He'd been gone for a total of seven hours—long enough to run his errands, see his uncle, and buy a dozen king-size beds.

Was there something else on his agenda? Something he hadn't told her about?

She thought about asking, and decided against it.

If Peter was keeping a secret, and if the secret concerned her, he would tell her when he was ready. Till then, he had a right to his privacy.

Over dinner, Peter described the bed he'd purchased, but Jenny paid scant attention. She was too caught up in her speculations.

If she'd written historical novels, like her friend Juno Jasperwall, she might have conjured up visions of Peter spending the afternoon in the arms of another woman. But Jenny wrote nonfiction, not romance, and she thought in less dramatic terms.

He told her about his visit to The Moutaineer, and it occurred to her he might have frittered away an extra hour or more looking at the camping gear, trying out fishing rods and comparing notes with the other ski buffs.

"The guy who worked on your skis wasn't in, so I spoke to the manager," Peter reported.

"What did he have to say?"

"About what you'd expect. He told me the bindings were loose, and I said, 'Thanks. I already knew that.'

Then I told him about your accident, and he asked if I'd leave the skis so he could have the fittings inspected, but he said far as he could tell they didn't look defective."

"So what did you do?"

"I left the damn skis. What else?" Peter's brusqueness made it clear that he hadn't been inclined to linger at the store.

Had he reacted the way he usually did when he felt out of sorts? Had he gone to the gym for a workout?

"Why didn't you tell me what happened with your car?" he demanded in the same rough tone.

"I thought I did."

"Not till two days after the fact."

"Well, I was going to tell you before we left for Tahoe, but it slipped my mind. We were busy getting ready for our trip, and I guess it just didn't seem important."

"Not important? How can you say that?"

"Because it wasn't, Peter. There was no damage done. None worth mentioning, at least. I wasn't hurt. Neither was the retaining wall, and you know how old the Toyota is. How often have you told me I ought to trade it in on a new car? Even if it's totaled, it's no big deal."

"It could've been a very big deal if the brakes had failed anywhere but in the driveway."

"But they didn't. And I don't understand why you're making an issue of this."

"Listen, Jenny, put yourself in my shoes. If I'd had two accidents in less than forty-eight hours, would you be concerned?"

"Naturally, but I wouldn't—"

The import of his question sank in and she fell silent. The idea that someone might have tampered with her bindings, with the brakes on her car, was preposterous. Who would want to hurt her? She had no enemies.

"They were *accidents,*" she insisted. "Surely you can't think otherwise. Even if they happened within forty-eight *minutes,* the timing's nothing more than unlucky coincidence."

"Unlucky, certainly. Coincidence?" Peter shook his head. "I hope to God that's all there is to it."

A chill of foreboding touched her spine. "If you're trying to frighten me, it's working."

"Aw, Jenny, that's the last thing I want! But I'd rather be safe than sorry. There's this mechanic I know who's a certifiable genius. He works on the Maserati. I stopped in and saw him this morning—"

"And you'd like him to go over my car? Very well. If it'll make you feel better."

"He's already picked it up."

"How'd he manage that without the keys?"

"I helped myself to the extra set, from the Peg-Board in the pantry."

She pushed her plate aside and began stacking the serving dishes. "Without my permission?"

"I didn't think you'd mind."

"Of course not," she said sharply. "Why would I?"

She tossed down her napkin as if it were a gauntlet, annoyed with Peter for presuming too much. But if the truth were told, she also felt relieved. At least now she knew why he'd been late coming home.

While he cleared the table, they talked about his visit to the office, about the rush of new clients the firm was representing, and the likelihood of Darien and Darien hiring an associate.

"It's the increase in bankruptcies," he said. "It hit when we were already snowed under. I brought home a couple of case files, and told Max I'd be in half days tomorrow and Friday."

"What about your vacation?"

"I'm afraid it'll have to wait till the workload's under control. If it's okay with you, I thought I'd get back to the old routine next week."

This announcement left Jenny speechless. As a rule, Peter was the most consistent of men. This morning he'd fretted about leaving her to fend for herself while he ran a few errands. Less than an hour ago he'd questioned whether her accidents were accidents at all. And now he was talking about leaving her alone full-time. Where was the consistency in that?

"What d'you say, honey?" Peter inquired. "Can you manage on your own?"

"I don't know why not. I've managed for the better part of twenty-seven years."

"Not with a broken ankle. There are certain things you can't do with your leg in a cast."

"So I've noticed, but I'm not planning on dancing *Swan Lake*."

"What about driving a car? Going up and down stairs? Getting yourself something to drink? I suppose you realize, you can't handle crutches and carry a mug of coffee."

Angry color pricked her cheeks. "There are taxis," she countered. "I've got a Thermos and a backpack. I'll carry my coffee in that. And if push comes to shove, I can sled downstairs on my fanny and crawl up."

"What about your new book? When do you have to get started on it?"

She darted a glance at him, her mind racing. Where were all these questions leading? Was he laying some sort of trap? "In a week or two," she answered warily. "There's no rush. The manuscript isn't due till the end of August, and I've already roughed out the opening chapters."

"How will you manage the research?"

Research. The fly in the ointment. The spoke in the wheel. Because research—her kind of research—required mobility, stamina, patience, attention to detail, an eagle eye . . . and two hands.

While not absolutely essential, the ability to drive a car helped.

How else could she transport a trunkful of resource materials home? And for as long as the crutches made getting around her own living room complicated, how could she keep appointments for interviews? How could she haul armloads of books up and down ladders and stairways, along miles of corridors, from the stacks to the checkout desk?

And what about the reference tomes that must be used on the library premises? Many of them were shelved in out-of-the-way crannies where no man had trod since heaven knew when.

Under normal circumstances, given an able-bodied writer, research caused eyestrain, headaches, backaches and other assorted ills.

Now and again, it also provided moments of pure joy.

Research was the aspect of writing Jenny liked best. And now the very thought of it made her feel defeated.

"Why are you cross-examining me?" She rapped her knuckles against the cast. "This chunk of concrete won't let me forget how limited I am. I don't need you to remind me. I'm painfully aware that I can't dance or go swimming or wear pretty shoes. I can't always scratch where I itch. Just getting dressed is a major operation—''

She faltered momentarily, as Peter jockeyed his chair toward hers and sat astride it. Scowling, she met his gaze.

"Do you think it's easy, not having the freedom to come and go as I please? Do you think it's easy, not being able to cope with the simplest chores?"

"No, sweetheart, I don't think anything of the sort. I know what you're going through. Believe me, I do. And I can appreciate how difficult it must be."

Do you? Jenny wondered. *I doubt it.* When he put a placating arm around her shoulders, she shook it off.

"Do you know what I had for lunch today? A deviled ham sandwich and tomato soup, that's what. I *hate* tomato soup! Rita practically force-fed me. She barged in and snooped and bullied and gossiped till I could feel my eyes glaze over, and short of physically throwing her out, there was nothing I could do to get her to leave. How do you think I felt, being at her mercy? Powerless, that's how. Useless."

"Please, honey, don't say that. Don't even think it. I never meant to criticize."

"Then why were you questioning me that way?"

"Because next week I'll be keeping regular office hours, and I don't like the idea of leaving you to your own resources all day." Peter slipped his arm about her again, and this time she didn't resist. "It's too soon, honey. Way too soon."

"But it can't be helped?"

"No, it can't."

"Will you be staying here nights?"

"Try to get rid of me."

"Well, then, I don't see the problem."

"The problem is, I know you, Jenny Spaulding. If you were drowning in quicksand, you wouldn't call for help. If someone offered a hand you might not refuse it, but you wouldn't ask for it, either." Peter gave her an eloquent look. "How am I doing so far? Am I right, or am I right?"

"You're right."

He tightened his hold on her, snugging her close to his side. "Don't get me wrong. I'm not saying pride and independence aren't wonderful traits. They are, and I love you for them. But there are times the combination gets a little scary."

"And this is one of them?"

"Exactly." His hand moved to the nape of her neck, settled there for a moment, strong and possessive, then massaged its way to the small of her back, soothing away knots of tension in the muscles along her spine.

"Mmm . . . feels good."

She arched into his touch, let her head loll to the side, and he nuzzled her ear. His breath stirred wisps of hair at her temple as he continued.

"The cast increases the risk. While you're in it, you should have someone available to help out when you need it. I wish that someone could be me, but since I can't be here, Betty Holtz came to mind. I thought you might ask her to stay with you."

"I couldn't, Peter. Betty already has a full schedule, with the classes she teaches and being dean of girls at Ringer-Dent."

"Would you consider asking Phyllis?"

"If I asked, I don't know how she'd get here. She's terrified of flying. The only way to get her on a cross-country flight would be to carry her aboard the plane, unconscious.''

Peter rested his chin against the crown of her head. "My mom's due back from Palm Springs next week. I don't suppose—''

"We're barely acquainted," Jenny broke in. "It's too big an imposition.''

She had seen Peter's mother several times over Christmas, and while their meetings had been cordial, the prospect of spending whole days alone with Lila Darien brought on an attack of cold feet. Especially now, when she wasn't at her best. When there was no way she could make a good impression.

Peter kissed her cheek, the angle of her jaw. "I figured you'd feel that way, which is why I went with Plan B.''

"Plan B?''

"My questions.'' His hand strayed along her rib cage, finding the most sensitive spots and working its magic. "I thought, if I could get you to admit you need help with your research, you might agree to hire an assistant.''

"A research assistant... That's an interesting idea, but I'm not sure it's practical. So much of research is stumbling across some nugget of information that's relatively unimportant but sparks your imagination. I'm not at all certain any two people would see the facts the same way.''

"Is there any reason someone else can't gather the material for you? Maybe even give it a preliminary screening?''

He closed her eyelids with kisses, then shifted his attention to her mouth. His lips brushed hers, knowing, persuasive, tasting and sampling, never quite settling, until his restraint became sweet torment. Until Jenny was willing to pay any price, if only he would kiss her properly.

"I guess it would depend on the person," she replied in a breathless murmur.

"She'd have to be compatible, that goes without saying."

"And thorough and bright and perceptive, and willing to work for the pittance I can afford to pay." Jenny looked at Peter through half-open eyes, focusing on his lips. "Assuming such a paragon exists, where would I find her?"

His mouth curved into a triumphant grin. "Why not let me take care of that?"

"On top of your own work? That hardly seems—"

Peter silenced her with a kiss. "Please, Jenny. Let me do this for you, if not for your own safety, for my peace of mind. Maybe I'm overreacting, but things have been so great between us, I can't help worrying. I don't want to lose what we have. I don't want to lose *you*. I'd like to prevent any more accidents."

His hands were busy with the buttons on her blouse. Her hands were tugging at his shirttail, tunneling beneath it. She could hear his heart pounding. Or was it her own? He solved the riddle of the fastener on her bra, and she sighed with pleasure.

"You win," she conceded.

With a haste that betrayed his eagerness, Peter rose and swept her up in his arms. "We both win."

He was right about this, as well, Jenny acknowledged as he strode toward the bedroom. Their argument didn't matter. She couldn't remember why she'd been upset with him in the first place, and she no longer cared who'd won.

If this was loss, it was sweeter than victory.

"WHAT WAS IT YOU SAID earlier about this bed not being big enough for both of us?" Jenny teased.

"What was it you said about being useless?" Peter responded in kind.

She rubbed her cheek against his shoulder, and walked her fingers through his chest hair. "I exaggerated."

"Is that what you call it?"

"Wouldn't you?"

"Nope. When you catch a ten-inch trout, and claim it's an eighteen-incher, that's an exaggeration. When you claim you can't do anything because your leg's in a cast, that's a whopper."

She touched him intimately, discovering his arousal. "Is that what you call it?"

"Wouldn't you?"

Laughing, Peter reached for her, and she smiled into the darkness. Later that night, utterly content, she fell asleep, still smiling.

THE TELEPHONE WOKE HER the following morning, even though Peter, already up and dressed for the day, answered on the second ring.

"It's for me," he said, when she opened one eye. "Go back to sleep."

"Mmph," she mumbled, and promptly drifted off again.

The next time she awoke it was after nine, the apartment was quiet and Peter was gone, but he'd left a tray on the nightstand. Covered dishes held servings of grapefruit and cereal, Thermos jugs contained milk and coffee.

She had finished eating and was pouring the coffee before she spotted the Valentine heart he'd drawn on her cast. Inside the heart was the inscription, "Peter loves Jenny." And beneath this, was another message.

From her perspective, it was upside down. She twisted this way and that, and had to resort to the use of hand mirrors, but at last she was able to make out the words, "Will you be my wife?"

Chapter Four

Given the right inducement, Jenny discovered she could get around much faster than she would have believed possible.

Instead of bothering with the crutches, she hopped from the bed to the telephone. She dialed the offices of Darien and Darien and asked to speak to Peter. The instant he came on the line she told him, "Yes!"

"You mean it, Jenny? You'll marry me?"

"Yes. Yes. *Yes!*"

"When?"

As soon as we can get the license, she thought. Then visions of the ceremony sprang to mind. It didn't have to be big or fancy, but she was traditionalist enough to want a church wedding.

She could see the altar, banked with candles. She could smell the flowers. Roses? No, camellias. And maybe a few daisies. She could hear the music and she could see Peter, tall and handsome, standing at the altar, and herself wearing something elegant—perhaps white lace?—walking down the aisle. . . .

Walking.

Not thumping. Not limping. Not clumping.

A broken leg didn't fit the picture. Neither did crutches.

"As soon as I'm out of this cast," she replied.

It seemed she was a romantic, after all.

She felt weird, wired, strangely buoyant, as she walked into Dr. Everett's office that Friday. During the three-week hiatus in her appointments with him, she was amazed to find herself missing their weekly sessions.

Much as she hated to admit it, it was fun matching wits with the old goat.

In the waiting room, she sipped stale coffee from a cardboard cup and thumbed through a year-old issue of People. *Before she read to the end of "Picks & Pans," the great man called her into his sanctum sanctorum. She headed straight for the sofa, but elected to sit rather than lie down.*

"Did you have a nice holiday?" she asked. "How was your trip to Belize?"

"Productive. Most productive. But we're here to talk about you."

Well, I guess that puts me in my place, she thought. Him doctor, me patient.

There was no room for confusion with a control freak like Everett. Everything he did was calculated to rain on her parade, burst her balloons and keep her from getting grandiose ideas. The way he rocked back in his chair, the way he perused her chart, even the way he stoked his pipe was a put-down.

His silence made her feel like climbing the walls, but she'd be damned if she'd let on.

She folded her hands in her lap, fixed her gaze on a speck on the wall, and began counting: One, one thousand...two, one thousand... *Silently, of course. She got to 156 before Everett spoke.*

"How have things gone for you since our last session?"

"Fine." *One fifty-seven...one fifty-eight...one fifty-nine...*

"My secretary tells me you called while I was away."

"I needed a refill on a prescription." *Gotta maintain the illusion that I'm taking my medicine, she thought. Besides, you never knew. The sleeping pills might come in handy sometime.*

"Ms. Lynch said you tried to reach me several times."

"Did she?" *One hundred sixty...one sixty-one...*

Everett peeled several messages off her chart and glanced through them. "Apparently, you were despondent. You were going through some sort of personal crisis. On Christmas Eve, wasn't it?"

She sat rigid, locked in stony silence, listening to the seconds tick by in her head.

"Wasn't Celia killed in a fire on Christmas Eve?"

One sixty-seven...one sixty-eight...

"Wasn't she your best friend? Your* only *friend?"*

One hundred seventy...one seventy-one...

"And her husband— What was his name?"

"Wyatt," *she said, in a small, tight voice.* "His name was Wyatt."

"Didn't he die a few days later?"

One seventy-five... Or was it one seventy-three? Where the hell had she left off?

"You know it's not uncommon to relive a tragedy on its anniversary date. Even to experience the shock, the sense of loss, we experienced when grief was fresh."

The lousy quack had made her lose count! There was a fifty-fifty chance she'd stopped counting on an odd number, which meant she'd have nothing but bad luck. If she'd stopped at one seventy-five, the numbers added up to thirteen—a double whammy of misfortune. The only one way to ward off catastrophe was to start over again and finish on eight-eight.

One, one thousand . . . two, one thousand . . .

"Then, too, at this time of year, we're constantly exhorted to get into the spirit of the season—"

"I wasn't despondent."

"Are you saying Ms. Lynch's report is inaccurate? You weren't depressed?"

"I was miffed, that's all. I found out Peter and his former girlfriend were going skiing over New Year's, but then he explained that they'd planned the trip long before he met me and I snapped right out of it."

"You're not jealous of this girlfriend?"

"Why should I be jealous? She's the past, I'm the present. Peter's fond of her, but he's in love with me."

"Yet she's the one he spent New Year's with."

"Only because he wanted to let her down gently. That's what a decent guy he is. Besides, when I think of how much she's lost, I feel kind of sorry for Jenny. She's a babe in the woods. No competition. Sooo sweet and innocent, if you know what I mean. Personally, I think it's an act."

Everett made a notation on her chart. "Why would you think that?"

"We all wear masks. You said so yourself. And the ingenue's an easy part to play. All it takes is youth and inexperience. No complexity. No verve. No mystery, either."

"I gather it's not your favorite role."

"*Obviously.*" She had strayed onto hazardous ground, but she couldn't wait to plunge ahead. "*I prefer a role with glamour and excitement.*"

"*The other woman, for instance?*"

"*If you want to call it that.*"

"*What would you call it?*"

"*The vixen, the vamp, the siren, the temptress. Take your pick.*"

"*I would not choose any of those names. They all have negative connotations.*"

"*The negatives are what makes them interesting, and give them an edge. They're characters who know how to command attention.*"

"*But not admiration.*"

"*Who cares? All the admiration in the world won't buy a cup of coffee.*"

The analyst gave a "*harumph*" of disapproval, and she shot him a withering look.

"*Let me tell you something, Doctor. The virtues of the ingenue pale into insignificance by comparison with the vices of the bad girl, because everyone—and I do mean everyone—is fascinated by evil.*"

"*That's quite a sweeping statement. It leaves no room for exceptions.*"

"*There are none.*"

"*Not even your young man?*"

"*No. Not even Peter.*"

Chapter Five

Although Rita paid daily visits, she didn't return Jenny's pen. When Jenny asked about it, Rita admitted she might have taken it home with her.

"If I did, I have no idea what happened to it. But since it means so much to you, I'll have a look around, see if I can find it."

That was Rita's last word on the subject, and even though the pen never showed up, Jenny chose not to pursue the issue. She wouldn't have mentioned the pen at all, if something else hadn't disappeared after each of Rita's calls.

None of the items was valuable or particularly exotic. An oven mitt on Thursday, a ladybug magnet on Friday, and on Saturday one of the seashells from Jenny's collection.

On Sunday Rita finally got to meet Peter, but they'd barely exchanged hellos when he excused himself to go jogging. And as she'd done on her first visit, Rita hung around till it was time to leave for work, waiting for him to get back.

Shortly after she left, Jenny noticed that some lilac-scented hand soaps were missing from the powder room.

"Rita strikes again," she told Peter that evening.

"You're sure she took the soap?"

"I'm positive, but I'll be darned if I can figure out why."

"She's probably a case of arrested development."

"Or a full-blown kleptomaniac," Jenny qualified. "But she can't possibly steal from everyone, so why does she take things from me?"

"What difference does it make *why* she takes things? What matters is, they're your things."

"But don't you see? If I knew why she does it, maybe I'd know how to put a stop to it."

"That part's easy," said Peter. "Next time she knocks at the door, don't let her in."

"That might work with most people, but not with Rita. She'd only keep knocking. She wouldn't go away. And I can't keep an eye on her every second she's here. She moves so much faster than I can."

"Then there's only one thing to do. Confront her with the truth. Tell her you're on to her. Tell her you don't associate with thieves."

"I couldn't, Peter. I have no proof. Even if I did, she lives just downstairs."

"All the more reason to nip this in the bud. If you let her get away with this, you'll only encourage her."

"You've got a point. But to call her a thief over a few bars of *soap?* That's more than confrontational. It's downright drastic. I'd feel like Captain Queeg counting strawberries."

Peter frowned and shook his head. "Do you think you'll feel any better if you wait till she takes something valuable?"

"I hope it won't come to that," Jenny replied.

And it didn't. At least, not immediately.

On Monday, Rita announced that from now on she'd be working days at the hospital. "I'm not a morning person," she said. "I like to sleep late, putter around the apartment a little, watch my serials. But starting tomorrow, I'll have to be on duty by seven-thirty. It's a bummer, and it's all Bev's fault."

"What does she have to do with it?" Jenny asked.

"She switched to working nights."

"So?"

"So the only reason we get along is 'cause we hardly ever see each other. If we worked the same shift, we'd be at each other's throats in a week."

Thank you, Beverly, for putting an end to my dilemma, Jenny thought. And then, because she was off the hook and could afford to be gracious, she offered to tape "General Hospital" for Rita.

That evening, Peter brought home a psychology text he'd picked up at the bookstore at Sacramento State: *Case Studies in Compulsive Behavior.*

"I thought this might help solve your problem with Rita," he explained.

"Thanks, love," Jenny said, smiling. "But it looks as if my problem has solved itself."

BEFORE HER ACCIDENT, Jenny had always kept busy. She'd had energy to burn and ambition to spare. The thing she'd been least good at was loafing. Yet now it seemed all she did most days was sleep.

She was taking a nap on the balcony the afternoon the king-size bed was delivered.

After she let the movers in, she returned to the balcony to keep out of their way while they removed the old bed and assembled the new one.

She sun was warm and the air balmy, more like April than the second week of January. In the apartment below, Bev Rudolph was playing the piano. The melody drifted on the breeze, romantic and poignant. Jenny couldn't identify the tune—not that she tried very hard. She let her thoughts drift with the music and lost track of time.

An hour might have passed, or it might only have been minutes before one of the workmen came out to say they were finished.

He handed her a clipboard with a sheaf of receipts attached, and asked her to sign on the lines marked with X's. "The bed's a beauty, ma'am. I think you're gonna be real happy with it."

"I'm sure I will be," Jenny answered, and although a niggling inner voice made her wonder if she should accept delivery of the bed sight unseen, she went ahead and signed the forms.

The mover scanned the papers over her shoulder. "One more thing. Do you want saltwater or fresh?"

Jenny stared at him, taken aback, chiding herself for not paying attention to Peter's description. Had he mentioned he'd bought a water bed?

"I—I don't know," she stammered. "Whichever's better, I guess."

"Truth is, there's advantages to both. But if it was me, I'd take salt."

"All right. Saltwater, it is, then."

The mover retrieved his clipboard and checked the appropriate boxes. "Don't worry about filling the tank or conditioning or any of that stuff. Our technician'll be along later to take care of it."

He issued these instructions over his shoulder, on his way to the door, and he was gone before Jenny could ask what he meant. She watched the delivery van negotiate the narrow horseshoe drive more puzzled than ever. She was about to collect her crutches so that she could take a look at the bed when Lila Darien arrived.

Jenny wished she'd had some advance notice of Lila's visit. She wished she had a few minutes to run a comb through her hair and splash cold water on her face—either salt or fresh. But instead of making herself more presentable, she pressed the intercom button to unlock the street door, then went out to meet Lila at the top of the stairs.

"I ran into your mail carrier in the lobby." Lila waved a handful of envelopes. "I asked for directions to your apartment and she asked me to give you these."

For Lila's benefit, Jenny produced a cheerful smile as she led the way to the apartment.

"Gracious! You handle those crutches like a pro."

A dubious skill at best, Jenny thought. But she kept on smiling.

"It's obvious you're feeling well," Lila said. "You look positively radiant!"

This was patently untrue, and Jenny knew it. She didn't feel radiant, nor did she look it. Lately, when she looked in a mirror, she saw a woman with a pale, drawn face and lackluster smile. A woman whose hair had lost its healthy bounce and whose eyes were dull and listless.

Peter's proposal had restored a trace of the sparkle, but only for a while, and since she and Peter had decided to keep their engagement to themselves for the time being, she didn't mention it. Instead, she went along with the charade.

"I've been getting lots of rest," she told Lila, "and the weather's been so nice, I've been spending most of the day on the balcony."

"Yes, I saw you out there when I drove in."

The opening bars of a Chopin nocturne rippled up from the apartment below, and after putting the mail on the coffee table, Lila followed the music to the sliding doors, where she paused to scan the banks of windows on the far side of the courtyard.

"You know what this reminds me of? That Hitchcock movie with Jimmy Stewart and Grace Kelly. The one where Jimmy's in a full-leg cast, confined to a wheelchair, and to pass the time he begins spying on his neighbors. In his inoffensive midwestern way, he becomes something of a voyeur, and then, by chance, he witnesses a murder."

"Thelma Ritter was in it," Jenny recalled.

"Yes. She was always such fun."

"Wasn't one of the neighbors a dancer? Sort of a party girl? And there was a songwriter, and a pair of newlyweds, and a couple with a little dog—"

"They slept on the fire escape because it was hot—or was that another couple?" Lila knitted her brows. "This is maddening. I know the title as well as I know my own name. It's right on the tip of my tongue—"

"*Rear Window,*" said Jenny.

"That's it! That ground-floor unit—the third from the end—would correspond to Miss Lonelyheart's. And the second floor windows kitty-corner to Miss Lonelyheart's . . . Those would belong to the killer."

Lila started as one of the windows opened and a frail dark-haired woman appeared in the aperture.

"As I live and breathe, it's Morticia Addams."

"She's actually the building manager. Her name's Toni Greer." It was warm in the sun, but all at once Jenny was shivering. She tried to force a laugh. "Would you like to sit inside or out?"

"Out," said Lila. "It's such a lovely view."

She opened the screen and stepped onto the balcony, and Jenny hopped after her, leaving the crutches inside. "Can I offer you some refreshments? Coffee or tea? Maybe some lemonade?" The nocturne had ended, and her voice sounded unnaturally loud in the silence.

"No thanks, dear. I just came from lunch with Max."

Jenny waited till her guest was seated, then stretched out on the lounger, studying the older woman. "Peter looks a lot like you," she remarked.

Lila flushed with pleasure. "Do you really think so?"

Jenny did. Both Peter and his mother had gold-flecked gray eyes that projected good-natured warmth, and both had grins that could be shy or bold, full of mischief or wonderment. Peter's grin was a bit lop-sided, while Lila's was softened by a dimple...and at the moment, somewhat uneasy.

"I should apologize for the surprise visit," she said, "but this is the way your mother wanted it. She insisted I drop in, unannounced."

"Phyllis insisted?"

"She's convinced you're keeping something from her, Jennifer. That you're not doing as well as you say you are."

"But she knows as much about my condition as I do. Peter's gone out of his way to keep her informed, and I've been in touch practically every day."

"I know, dear. She told me you've been conscientious about writing, but she's your mother. No matter how old you are, or how conscientious, nothing will ever change that. And she was terribly anxious. She had to do something, to be certain you're all right."

"So she dragged you into it, asked you to check up on me."

"On the contrary. She didn't have to ask. I offered to pay you a visit, for reasons of my own."

"Because of Peter," Jenny said softly. "Because you're his mother."

"I wouldn't have put it so bluntly, but that's about the size of it." Smiling, Lila continued, "You see, Jenny, I know how Peter feels about you. And unless I'm mistaken, you feel the same way about him."

"I love him, Mrs. Darien. I don't mind telling you that."

"But you don't feel comfortable with me, do you, dear? If you did, you'd call me something less formal than 'Mrs. Darien.'"

Jenny stirred the air with one hand, groping for a response. "I— The truth is, I don't know you very well."

"Nor I you, but I'd like to."

"So would I."

"Then I'd say it's time we got better acquainted. Wouldn't you?"

"Yes. Only I'm not sure how to go about it."

"I could begin by telling you a little about myself. Details Peter may not have mentioned, that you may be able to identify with. Did you know, for instance, that my father was in the foreign service?"

"No, I didn't."

"Dad was a career attaché, not a diplomat, not one of the elite. He wasn't wealthy and he didn't have enough clout to rise to the level of ambassador, but I grew up around embassies just the same. I cut my teeth on affairs of state. I mastered the ins and outs of protocol."

Lila leaned back in her chair and stared at the treetops, as if they contained images from the past. "By the time I entered my teens I'd lived in ten countries on three continents, and I was accustomed to people of influence. More than that, I felt at home with them. I could hobnob with the intelligentsia, with industrialists and cabinet ministers, and never turn a hair. But in spite of my cosmopolitan upbringing, there came a time when I was overwhelmed by the thought of meeting a woman most of my crowd would have dismissed as an ordinary housewife."

"Your husband's mother," Jenny murmured.

"Absolutely. I wanted so much for her to like me, I worked myself into a tizzy. I was afraid she wouldn't approve of me, that she'd see me as a rival for Bradley's affection, that she'd try to come between us, that she'd do everything in her power to undermine our relationship."

Lila lapsed into silence and slanted a glance Jenny's way. "Does any of this strike a familiar chord?"

Jenny sighed. "All of it does, to one degree or another. But it's no reflection on you. You've been awfully nice. The soul of kindness, in fact. It's just that I'm a worrier."

"You have that in common with your mother."

Jenny admitted this was true. "Among other things."

"Such as?"

"My conscience."

A twinkle leaped into Lila's eyes. "Won't let you get away with much, will it?"

"Won't let me get away with *anything*," Jenny replied.

"Well, dear, look at the bright side. You've inherited your father's talent as a journalist...and of course, his appearance."

Jenny looked at Lila, surprised. "I didn't realize you'd met my father."

"Oh, yes, many times, dating back to his freshman year at Stanford. Gareth and Max were great chums, you know, and Brad had just been posted—I forget exactly where. I doubt the country exists anymore. Anyway, Peter was only a toddler, so we stayed behind, at our house in Burlingame. It wasn't far from the campus, and most weekends Max and Gareth would show up."

"What was he like in those days?"

"Bright. Witty. Happy-go-lucky. Full of the dickens. The total opposite of Max, who's always been a stick-in-the-mud. I suppose that's why they got along so well. Gareth used to prod Max out of his rut, and Max was a steadying influence for Gareth."

Lila smiled reminiscently. "Things came easily to your father, Jenny. He seemed to love everyone, and everyone loved him. Peter and I. My in-laws. Every female between the ages of eight and eighty. And men liked him, too. He was a real charmer."

"Phyllis would agree with that. She used to accuse my father of getting by on charm and leaving others to pick up his tab."

"Meaning the two of you," Lila said thoughtfully. "I can see why your mother would feel that way, but I'd be interested in hearing what you think."

"I think he and Phyllis had different needs. He liked being on the move, but she wanted to settle down. So he tried things her way. He tried to be a responsible family man. He wasn't very good at it, but that doesn't mean he didn't love us. In his own way, I think he did. More than my mother ever realized."

"I'd say that's a pretty fair analysis," Lila replied. "I know how proud he was of you. The last time I saw him, he showed me a composition you'd written. I don't recall what it was about. How you'd spent your summer vacation or something like that. But I'll never forget the expression on Gareth's face as he removed your theme from his billfold. And the way he handled it...so carefully, taking such pains to keep the paper from getting crinkled."

"When was this?" Jenny inquired.

"Almost twenty years ago."

"In Santa Marta?"

Lila nodded. "It was toward the end of the war there...only a week or two before the capital fell. Bradley had been a captive of the rebels for more than a year. They were holding him at their stronghold near the Rio Seco, and your father had been there. He'd seen Bradley. He'd actually spoken to him. And when Gareth left the rebel encampment, he managed to smuggle a message past their leader—"

"Jaime de Silva."

A shadow of pain crossed Lila's face at the mention of the man who had engineered her husband's kidnapping and eventual murder.

"I understand you've written a book about de Silva," she said.

"*Diary of a Revolutionary,*" Jenny replied. "It's the second book in my Santa Marta trilogy. The first is *Diary of a Journalist*. It's about my father. And the third book's—"

"About Bradley," Lila finished. "Does it have a title?"

"Diary of a Diplomat." Jenny cleared her throat. "I hope I can do him justice."

She studied the older woman, trying to gauge her reaction. But for the moment Lila seemed more interested in the scene that was unfolding in the manager's apartment than she was in her late husband's biography.

"What *is* that woman doing?"

Jenny looked toward the open window, where Toni Greer could be seen placing an ornate silver candle holder at the center of table draped in black.

"It looks as if she's getting ready for a séance."

"A *séance!*"

"She has them regularly. I gather she has quite a reputation as a medium, and quite a following."

"Well, I never . . ." Lila rose and moved to the handrail for a clearer view. "You mean she goes into a trance? Talks a lot of mumbo jumbo? Calls up her spirit guide and communicates with the dead?"

"I really couldn't say. I've never been to one."

"I should hope not!"

Toni was smoothing her hands over the tablecloth, straightening the fringed edging. She struck a match and lighted the candle while Lila watched with horrified fascination.

"This is incredible, even for California," she murmured, sinking back into her chair. "In 1950, when Bradley and I came out to visit his parents, the first thing we saw when we left the train station was a mob of people wearing bed sheets. I gawked at them because I assumed they were Klansmen, but nobody else paid any attention, and I don't mind telling you, I was shocked. I'd always thought of California as a haven for liberals. But then Bradley told me the people in sheets weren't political at all. They were some sort of religious cult. Looking back, I imagine that should have been more shocking, but at the time it only seemed colorful."

"An appropriate introduction to the state," said Jenny.

"Yes. Definitely. Anything goes in California. I know that. I've traveled around the world. I like to think I'm fairly sophisticated. And now that I've lived here forty years, I should be shockproof. But a séance, for heaven's sake? That's...well, it's medieval! I thought they'd gone the way of rumble seats and...and corsets."

"Haven't you heard?" Jenny asked lightly. "Corsets are making a comeback."

"Thanks to Madonna, no doubt."

"No doubt," Jenny agreed. "Chances are, if she wore a straitjacket, they'd be all the rage."

"If you'd ever worn a corset, you'd know it amounts to the same thing." Lila rolled her eyes, despairing. "Why do we do it, Jennifer? Why do we let rock musicians and Hollywood starlets dictate what we wear? So many things that become the height of fashion are in the most deplorable taste, yet we'll stand in line to buy them. We'll wear earrings the size of hubcaps...shoes that hurt our feet.... Why do women go to such lengths to keep up with the latest fad? Are we really such sheep?"

Peter's neon cacti and his Nike cross trainers came to mind, and Jenny smiled. "It's not just women," she said.

"No, come to think of it. Men are as gullible as we are, bless them, but somehow, that isn't much comfort." Sighing, Lila watched Toni Greer arrange chairs about the table. "Why is she wearing gloves?"

"She always wears gloves. White ones. There are several schools of thought about the reason for them."

The answer came in a stage whisper, from directly beneath the balcony. The instant they heard it, Lila and Jenny looked over the railing at the slender thirty-something blonde, who was standing on the ground-floor patio, not the least bit abashed that she'd been caught eavesdropping.

"Some say it's an affectation," she continued without inflection, peering up at them with intent, brooding eyes. "Others say it's an aberration, and my roommate, who reduces everything to the lowest common denominator, says Toni wears gloves so she won't leave fingerprints."

Lila glanced from the blonde to Toni Greer, then back to the blonde again. "What do you say, Miss—"

"Rudolph, isn't it?" Jenny spoke up. "Beverly Rudolph?"

"That's right," she replied, unsmiling. "And you're Jennifer Spaulding."

Jenny nodded agreement and introduced Peter's mother, who urged Beverly to go on.

"You were saying?" Lila prompted.

"I was about to say that Toni's eccentric. In the six months I've known her, she's exhibited many quirks, most of which haven't lasted. But I've never seen her without gloves and long sleeves, even on the hottest days last summer, which leads me to believe their purpose is strictly cosmetic."

"In other words, she's hiding something," Lila summarized. "Have you a theory as to what it might be?"

"My guess would be scars. Her husband was killed when their house burned. He was pinned beneath some debris, she tried to save him and barely escaped with her life."

"How tragic," said Lila.

"Yes, it is," Beverly replied. "So you see, the séances are Toni's way of coping with her husband's death. There's nothing sinister about her. She's an extremely private person. She's uncomfortable with crowds, so she rarely goes out. She's borderline pathologically shy, and I think her shyness is related to her psychic gifts. When she's with other people, she can't help picking up vibes—"

"Surely you're not saying she's a mind reader," Lila broke in. "You can't honestly believe that she intercepts thought waves and sees the future."

"Why not, Mrs. Darien? Stranger things have happened."

"But you seem like a rational person."

"Rational enough to believe my own eyes. I've attended a séance or two. I've heard Toni's predictions. They're quite specific, and I've never known her to be wrong."

"Even if you've seen her in action, you can't be certain there's no trickery involved."

Beverly offered a shrug and a thin, mechanical smile. "It's easy to condemn things you don't understand, but before you judge her too harshly, think how difficult it is for her, trying to sort out reams of sensory data. Think of the strain she's under, having a window into the future, seeing illness and death—all manner of suffering—and knowing there's nothing she can do to prevent it. Think what a burden it must be."

Burden wasn't a bad definition for the precognitive skills Beverly described, although, as Jenny was beginning to realize, the word *curse* might be more appropriate.

If the events Toni prophesied often came to pass, her gift must be a heavy burden for everyone concerned. Well nigh intolerable for Toni herself, and even less tolerable for the poor unfortunates whose futures she forecast.

Chapter Six

There's a threat hanging over you. An aura of danger thick as a cloud...

Beverly might consider this prediction "quite specific," but Jenny didn't. Not nearly specific enough. Even the process of elimination didn't narrow it down.

If the threat had nothing to do with skiing, if it led to consequences more serious than her scrape with the car, what could it involve?

Practically anything, that's what.

Natural disasters. Acts of God. Fire, flood, earthquakes, pestilence. An illness. A household accident. Or some freak mishap. A fall in the bathtub. A plane crashing into her apartment. The possibilities were endless.

Toni hadn't even specified whether the threat was physical. It could be emotional, financial, professional.

And she'd set no time limit. "Don't take unnecessary risks," she'd said. But for how long?

Does she know? Jenny wondered. If I asked, would she tell me, "This warning expires at midnight on January 31?"

And the bit about the threat coming from a stranger was so hackneyed, it was ludicrous. Did Toni actually expect her to buy it? Just thinking that she might made Jenny feel indignant.

For two cents she'd tell Toni to clean up her act. To get real, get a life, or at least get some fresh material. Some *logical* material, for heaven's sake.

Jenny was a newcomer to the city. A newcomer to the neighborhood. A newcomer to the apartment complex. With the exception of Peter and one or two others, she was surrounded by strangers. Literally. Rita and Bev downstairs, a personnel manager next door, a couple of flight attendants across the corridor, and in the opposite direction, across the courtyard, Toni Greer.

And since Jenny had no enemies, if there *was* a threat, who else would it come from but a stranger? Certainly not a friend! And not Peter's mother, who seemed friendly enough when she left.

A few minutes later the technician arrived—another stranger, of course—to finish installing the bed. He spent an hour or more puttering about, but Jenny was too busy fuming to pay attention to what he was doing.

Not long after his departure, Peter got home. The moment he walked through the door, he asked, "Did they deliver the bed?"

"Yes, they did."

Grinning like a kid on Christmas morning, he made a beeline for the bedroom. "Hey, this is great! It's even better than I thought it would be."

His excitement was contagious. In spite of her distraction, Jenny was not immune. She grabbed the crutches and hurried after Peter, only to halt, abruptly, in the doorway.

"What do you think, honey? Isn't this headboard something?"

It was something, all right, but she wasn't sure what. "I've never seen anything like it," she said. Not in her wildest dreams.

Peter's taste in furniture ran to minimalist designs, where form followed function. She had expected him to choose something modern, with clean, simple lines; she had hoped he'd choose something in teak.

Something that would blend with the sampler motif in the area rug. Something that would go with the oval pier glass whose dark mahogany frame was carved with vine leaves and grapes. Something that would go with the mauve slipper chair and the walnut bookcase and the reproduction Tiffany lamps.

But what he'd chosen didn't go with anything.

The headboard was a hodgepodge of chromium and shiny black Lucite framing beveled sheets of glass, which formed a tank filled with water, capped with a slab of black Lucite—

"They make football helmets out of this stuff." Peter gave the headboard an affectionate pat. "Sturdy as hell. Built to take a lot of punishment, and last a lifetime."

Terrific, thought Jenny. *Just what I needed.*

Her gaze wandered back to the water-filled tank in the headboard, registering the layer of white gravel blanketing the bottom, noticing shells and rocky grottoes, lacy branches of coral....

"It's an aquarium!"

"Also a work of art," Peter qualified. "This setup has everything."

Everything but fish. Unless they were hiding.

She moved closer to the bed, searching for residents in the aquarium, while Peter bounced on the edge of the innerspring mattress, testing it for comfort.

"You've gotta try this, honey."

He sprawled diagonally across the bed, stretching his arms and legs to show her how roomy it was, then rolled onto his stomach and pointed out the amenities of the aquarium: the heater and aerator, the filtration system, the gauges that measured water temperature and salinity.

"The lights are on a rheostat." He turned the dimmer knob to demonstrate. "Isn't that nifty?"

Jenny cleared her throat, stalling. Peter looked so thrilled with his purchase, so pleased with himself. She hadn't the heart to hurt his feelings, but for the life of her she couldn't think of anything complimentary to say.

She settled for noncommittal. "It's certainly unique."

"It's one of a kind, all right." The lift of his eyebrows told her that she would not get off the hook so easily.

"I'm stunned," she ventured, trying for more enthusiasm. "Really, Peter. I don't know when I've been so surprised."

"Wait'll you see it with fish in it."

"When will that be?"

"They'll be delivered as soon as the habitat's stable. Probably Monday."

Oh, joy! A few days' grace. When the bedroom was dark, she wouldn't have to look at the headboard, but there was no way she could ignore the aquarium.

"Is the aerator always this noisy?" she asked. "I mean, won't it be hard to sleep with it bubbling like that?"

Peter waved a dismissive hand. "Is the ocean too noisy? Does it keep you awake or is it relaxing?"

"It's relaxing, but—"

"So's an aquarium. Take my word for it. This little beauty's better than a sedative."

But it wasn't. Not for her, at any rate.

Peter spent the evening doodling in the margins of a pet-shop catalog, choosing the fish for the aquarium. That night, he slept like a baby. She, on the other hand, lay scowling into the darkness, trying not to listen to the aerator. But the harder she tried, the more obtrusive it became. Soon she could separate the noise it made into distinctive components.

The rushing hiss of bubbles was loudest. Even burrowing beneath the pillow didn't eliminate the sound, which was maddening as a dripping faucet and set her teeth on edge.

Slightly less maddening was the chugging whir of the pump, and faintest of all was the background hum of electricity.

At 1:00 a.m., snuggling close to Peter, she tried to mask these alien sounds with the restful sound of his breathing.

It didn't work.

One-fifteen found her flailing about, wondering why she had pretended she liked the headboard. Why hadn't she told Peter the truth when she'd had the chance? Now it was too late; she was stuck with the bed.

Wishing that he could share her misery, she delivered a well-aimed kick toward his shins.

That didn't work, either.

Peter turned over and muttered something unintelligible, but he didn't wake up.

At one-thirty, still tossing and turning, she began praying for a power failure.

Nothing happened. The electricity hummed. The pump went *chuggawhirr, chuggawhirr.* The air bubbles hissed, sizzled and popped, and insomnia tightened its grip.

At one-forty-five, resigned to a night without sleep, Jenny rolled out of bed, fumbled into her robe, and picked her way along the hall to the living room. Once there, wrapped in blessed quiet, she stood at the balcony door, looking at Toni Greer's dark, silent windows across the courtyard, while her thoughts strayed backward in time.

There's a threat hanging over you. An aura of danger...

"Idiot," Jenny berated herself. "Don't get started on that again."

After drawing the drapes, she moved away from the sliding door, heading for the couch. She paused along the way to turn on a lamp and find something to read. The first thing that came to hand was the *Case Studies* book Peter had bought. It wasn't the light diversion she'd had in mind, but the cover notes and teaser captured her interest.

"Might as well give it a try. Maybe I'll learn something."

Her decision made, Jenny lounged back against the sofa cushions and started to read.

An hour later she was still reading, discovering bits and pieces of herself and everyone she knew in the histories of patients who were afflicted with obsessive/compulsive disorder.

Her mother's phobias, for instance.

Phyllis was afraid of flying, afraid of being abandoned, afraid of death, afraid of growing old. Which, if one thought about it, didn't leave her many options. She used a rinse on her hair to hide the gray, insisting, "There is nothing wrong with a person making the most of her appearance."

There was nothing unusual in that, of course. Jenny supposed the majority of middle-aged women would agree with her mother. But Phyllis carried her campaign against aging several steps further than most.

She lied about her age. She lied about Jenny's. What's more, she treated Jenny like a ten-year-old, which was her way of lying to herself. In the last few years she'd had a tummy tuck, liposuction, breast augmentation and a face-lift—not out of vanity, as Jenny had once assumed, but out of fear.

Whatever anxieties drove her, however, Phyllis's case was far from clinical.

She had her house and garden, hobbies, a thriving career, a busy social life. Her pursuit of youth might be worrisome to her daughter and expensive for her. At times it might be inconvenient, but as compulsions went, it was relatively mild.

As for Betty Holtz's superstitions, they were little more than a habit, as were Lila Darien's globe-trotting, Juno Jasperwall's systematized way of picking titles for her books, and the lengths to which Jenny herself would go to ensure that she finished a manuscript with the same two or three pencils she'd used to start it.

The same could be said of the ritual Peter went through whenever he served at tennis. He'd tighten his shoelaces, pull up his socks, inspect the strings of his racket, then test it by bouncing the ball, not once or twice, but *three* times. Invariably. As if he were invoking the gods of the court. And only then would he serve.

According to *Case Studies,* the beliefs and behaviors encountered in obsessive/compulsive disorder are idiosyncratic, complex, intense and consuming. In moderate cases, the malady interferes significantly with the patient's life. In severe cases, a great deal of the patient's energy and most of his day are spent resisting compulsions, concealing them, or acting upon them. At that point, the disorder becomes incapacitating.

An appendix in the text outlined a dozen or more common obsessions. One near the top of the list caught Jenny's eye. In extreme instances, fear of contamination led to a refusal to pick up objects bare-handed and to repeated, incessant washing.

The classic Lady Macbeth syndrome, except that guilt wasn't necessarily a factor.

But what about Toni Greer? What if she wore gloves not to conceal burn scars as Beverly Rudolph had theorized, but to conceal a fear of touching things, of soiling her hands?

Or perhaps to conceal the guilt she felt because of her husband's death?

Given the manner of his death, it wouldn't be surprising, as Jenny had cause to know. Hadn't she suffered pangs of conscience after her father's murder? Hadn't she condemned herself for not realizing how desperate he was? How many times had she told herself, "If only we'd been closer, I might have been able to save him?"

The truth was, she still blamed herself for the part she'd played in their estrangement. For all her sins of omission. For the things she hadn't done.

She should have written her father more often. She should have made more of an effort to keep in touch. And she had never told him she loved him. She would always regret that. She'd managed to keep her failures in perspective, but she hadn't done it by herself.

In her time of grief, Peter had given her solace. In her time of despair, he had given her hope. He had seen her fears and bolstered her courage. He had seen her guilt and offered absolution.

But who would absolve Toni?

From what Jenny had seen, she had no family, no friends, no confidants. With no one to offer comfort, no one to tell her it was not her fault that she had survived her husband, she'd fallen into a state of perpetual mourning.

She held séances and she wore white gloves. *Always.* Perhaps they hid her shame, but they might also provide a symbolic barrier to her feelings.

If all one felt was the pain of guilt, wouldn't it be better to feel nothing?

Jenny marked her place and closed the book, yawning and rubbing one hand across her eyes. They felt so heavy, she could scarcely keep them open. She let them drift shut and rested her head against the back of the couch....

The next thing she knew it was morning and Peter was standing over her, dressed for the office, fanning the steam from a mug of coffee her way.

"Mmm, smells good." The aroma coaxed her to a sitting position, and Peter set out a coaster and handed her the mug. "I could get used to this, you know. Having you serve me coffee in bed."

"Only you're not in bed."

"Couldn't sleep," she said.

Last night she would have complained about the aerator, but this morning her mood was more mellow. She was willing to concede that other things had contributed to her insomnia. Too long a nap yesterday afternoon, for example, and too many things on her mind.

In the kitchen, the toaster popped up, and Peter went off to see about breakfast. In minutes he was back with a pitcher of orange juice and a plate of English muffins. He spread the food on the coffee table, returned to the kitchen for glasses and napkins, then sat on the hassock, facing her. He was pouring the juice when he spotted the book that, sometime during the night, had slipped to the floor.

"I see you've been doing some reading," he said. "Did you learn anything about our light-fingered friend?"

"Not really. Kleptomaniacs may have uncontrollable urges but I'm not sure they're in the same category as obsessive/compulsives."

Jenny made a droll face to punctuate her answer, and Peter leaned forward and captured her mouth with his. "When you do that I have an uncontrollable urge to kiss you."

She gave him a guileless stare. "Do what?"

"Wrinkle your nose like that."

"Like this?" She repeated the gesture.

He kissed her again, and this time her arms went around him. Her lips clung to his.

"You're a tease, Jenny Spaulding, and I love it."

"Yes," she said gravely. "I know you do."

He helped himself to one of the muffins. "I'm going to do some shopping on my way home. Is there anything I can pick up for you?"

"Some earplugs."

"So the aerator *did* bother you."

"Give me a few nights. I'll get used to it." She took a sip of juice. "If you're anywhere near an office-supply store, I could use some legal pads."

"Those I can get at the office. At a discount." He ate some of his muffin, then did a belated double take. "What do you need legal pads for?"

The guileless look came back into play. "Notes. Outlining. Rough drafts—"

"You've decided to start my dad's book."

"Yes, I have."

"Have you thought about hiring an assistant?"

Another stranger, Jenny thought. Heart sinking, she asked, "Do you have a candidate in mind?"

Peter nodded. "Her name's Delores Chapin. She's about your age, give or take a few years, working on her master's in English at Sacramento State."

"So she knows her way around a library."

"Absolutely. If you'd like to interview her, Dee said she'd be happy to stop by."

"No strings attached?"

"All I ask is that you meet her." Peter broke into a grin so broad it seemed incandescent, so warm it touched her heart. "C'mon, honey. What've you got to lose?"

When he put it that way, how could she refuse?

Another Friday, another appointment with the shrink. Only this one was different. The moment she saw Everett, she sensed a transformation.

The change was subtle, nothing overt. At first glance he seemed as smug and complacent as ever, as full of bluff and bluster and hot air. Anyone less perceptive might have considered him the same paternalistic windbag, but she was not easily fooled.

She saw the tremor in his hands, the film of sweat on his brow. She heard the uneasiness in his voice, and noticed the way he studied her—as if she were a bug under a microscope.

His watchfulness underscored his change of attitude.

At last week's session, she'd gotten carried away. She'd let off some steam and given him a peek at certain truths about herself. Truths that must have prompted him to take another look at her case, and to reevaluate the way he'd handled it. In the process he'd probably seen himself in a less than flattering light, and now his confidence was shaken. He was riddled with doubt.

The balance of power had shifted to her! She knew this intuitively and exulted in it. But she was careful not to let on.

Much as she resented being treated as an inferior, she would rather be in therapy than in prison, and if she provoked Everett, if she displayed contempt or challenged his authority, prison would be the next stop.

So she didn't argue with his suggestion that it might be wise to explore her reactions to Celia's death.

"You're the doctor," she said. "Only I'm not sure raking over the past will do any good. 'Specially when it's been so long."

Five years might seem the blink of an eye to a burned-out old fogy like Everett, but to her the incidents surrounding Celia's death were as remote as ancient history. And like ancient history, they might have happened to someone else.

She was tempted to protest, to say that she'd been a different person then, with an entirely different identity, but she didn't. She didn't quibble, even when Everett replied with a preachy, "It's never too late to work through the stages of grief."

Stages of grief? What a crock! *But it was typical of Everett. He actually believed there was something to be gained from analyzing emotions. From naming them. Defining them. Quantifying rage and anguish and sorrow, as if they could be measured and weighed like potatoes.*

"Once you've confronted your feelings," he said, "honestly, without holding back, you won't need to vent them in senseless acts of violence."

This was a veiled reference to a more recent fire. A blaze she had deliberately set. It had been extinguished when it was little more than a flicker, with minor damage to the files of a former employer.

At the time, she had intended to torch the whole damned building; a fire had seemed fitting punishment for the man who had fired her.

Unfortunately she'd been caught red-handed, as it were. She'd been reprimanded, patronized and threatened with arrest, and she in turn had wept, confessed her crime and thrown herself on his mercy.

"I don't know what got into me," she'd sobbed. "I haven't been myself lately. I can't sleep ... can't eat ... can't think. Some nights, all I do is cry. I wish I had the courage to kill myself. I'm lonely. So lonely. Oh, God, I want to die!"

After this stellar performance, her employer agreed not to press charges. Instead, he had delivered her to Dr. Everett's custody. But not until she'd written a confession.

"I'll keep a copy of this," he'd said. "The original will go to my lawyer. It will remain confidential as long as you keep your nose clean, stay away from me and cooperate with the doctor. However, if you choose not to cooperate, a copy goes to the police. If you don't keep your distance, a copy goes to the police. If you set any fires, a copy goes to the police. If you ever step out of line, if you contact my staff or any member of my family, if you're caught shoplifting or jaywalking, a copy goes to the police. If lightning should strike my office or my home, God forbid, or if anything happens to me before you're formally dismissed from treatment, a copy of your confession will go to the police."

After a pause for dramatic effect, he'd concluded, "Do you understand these conditions? Have I made myself clear?"

He had. Painfully. Degradingly.

She understood that he had tried her, found her guilty and imposed a sentence that made Dr. Everett her probation officer and himself warden in absentia.

Her prison had no bars, but it was a prison nonetheless.

He'd made her sign a release so that Everett could send him progress reports. He monitored her activities at work, at home—his spies were everywhere. There was no way to avoid his surveillance. She would have had more privacy in jail.

There were times when she wished she could turn herself over to the police and get it over with, but she couldn't risk an official investigation. She was forced to comply with his demands.

For more than fifteen months she had toed the mark and marked time, waiting for the day when she could get even. She had kept her biweekly appointments with

Dr. Everett—every Tuesday and Friday, regular as clockwork. She'd lain on his couch, invented a history, followed his instructions, listened to his lectures, and taken his pills....

Until the night last December when it suddenly occurred to her that Everett was a hopeless incompetent, and that the warden was as crafty and vindictive as she.

That was when she realized her sentence would never end. There would be no parole. No pardon. No time off for good behavior.

The only way out of her prison was to break out. Or else to die trying.

Well, why not? she'd told herself. You've done it before.

The next morning she'd gone off her medication.

Ten days later she'd seen Peter Darien.

The following week she'd learned who he was, and within hours of this discovery she'd tracked him to Jennifer Spaulding's apartment.

It was there that she experienced the final revelation. Seeing them together, she knew that she'd found something far more vital than a man who attracted her, something more exciting and unexpected than a replacement for Wyatt.

She had found a means of escape.

Chapter Seven

Jenny began going through her files that morning, assembling the data she'd gathered for Bradley Darien's biography. By late afternoon, when Dee Chapin arrived, the work had spilled out of her office into the living room. Drifts of paper covered the tables, the chairs, the sofa, the floor.

"Wow! You really do need help getting organized." Dee's horrified expression made it clear that tact was not one of her strong points. But it was equally clear that she had other things going for her. A knockout figure. Titian hair. Big green eyes most men would die for.

Jenny accepted the resumé Dee offered, wondering why Peter hadn't mentioned how striking she was. Surely he must have noticed.

"I should apologize for the mess," Jenny said. "Things aren't usually this chaotic. It's just that I've been sorting my notes."

"Don't apologize, Jennifer, and please don't be embarrassed. I understand completely. I've been around creative people all my life. I know that when you're focused on your work, you couldn't care less about your surroundings."

Dee's smile brought dimples to her cheeks and a hot rush of color to Jenny's. She hadn't been embarrassed before, but now she was. And irritated. With Delores Chapin and herself.

She's the one who's looking for a job, Jenny thought. I don't have to justify myself to her.

"I don't want to give you the wrong impression," Dee went on earnestly, her smile wavering, her voice wobbling. "I'm inclined to be neat, but I'm not a fanatic about it, and I'm sorry if I offended you. I shouldn't have said anything. I hear these stupid remarks coming out of my mouth, and I can't believe I'm *saying* them. It's an awful habit—the bane of my existence—but I can't seem to break it. Whenever I'm nervous, I rattle on."

"Why are you nervous?"

"Because the chance to work with you means so much to me. It's the chance of—"

"Wait a minute," Jenny pleaded, holding up one hand. "Did Peter tell you the job's temporary?"

"Yes, he did."

"And you discussed salary?"

Dee nodded eagerly. "He also told me you're working on his father's biography. That's so thrilling. And romantic. I only hope the hours don't conflict with my class schedule."

"Which is?"

"I have seminars that meet Tuesday and Thursday mornings, and I teach a freshman English class Friday afternoons."

"That shouldn't be a problem," said Jenny. "My routine's fairly flexible. In fact, you can more or less set your own hours. Toward the end of the manuscript there may be occasions when I'll need the answer to some question or the other *yesterday,* but that's months away. Probably not till summer.''

"Once the semester's over, my time is yours.''

"How are you with details?''

"They're my forte. I have the kind of mind that retains little-known facts—the more arcane, the more vividly I remember them.'' Dee hesitated and smiled almost wistfully. "I realize this is a part-time job we're talking about, not a potential career, but it's the learning experience I find interesting. Opportunities like this don't come along every day of the week. Or maybe they do for some people, but not for me.''

Jenny scooped a stack of papers off one of the chairs. "Have a seat, take a deep breath, and we'll start over again. Only this time, forget you're being interviewed. Pretend I'm a friend or a teacher—''

Dee shook her head. "You're too young to be a teacher.''

"That'll win you brownie points.''

Jenny cleared a chair for herself and skimmed Dee's one-page resumé, which outlined her educational and employment backgrounds, and listed personal references.

"I see you're from southern California,'' Jenny said. "What brought you to Sacramento?''

"My ex-husband. We met at UCLA, and after graduation we moved up here. He went to work as an accountant for the Franchise Tax Board and I enrolled at Sacramento State. The marriage didn't last long, though. We were both so young. Neither of us was ready to settle down and all we did was fight. We couldn't agree about anything. If one of us said, 'It's a nice day,' it was likely to set off another battle. Eventually he started seeing someone else, and they drifted into an affair. After that, divorce was inevitable. But so far it's been fairly friendly.''

"You still see each other?''

"Now and then. Maybe two or three times a year. My ex has been very supportive. I still care about him and I think he cares about me.''

"Is that why you've stayed on?''

"Only partly.'' Dee faltered and glanced away from Jenny. "I come from a long line of overachievers. After my marriage failed, I couldn't go home without some success under my belt.''

Jenny cleared her throat. "I appreciate your candor, but just now I'd like to get back to something you mentioned earlier...about working with creative people.''

"I haven't exactly worked with them. I've *lived* with them. My father's an architect, my mother's a screenwriter, my sister's a set designer with Universal Studios and my kid brother's a musician.''

"Quite an accomplished family. You must be proud of them.''

"Yes, and a bit envious of their talent. I'd give anything to be able to write professionally, or paint or play an instrument, and they all seem to take their gifts for granted.''

"I suspect the ability to live with so many artists is a talent in itself.''

"I don't know about that, but it takes a willingness to compromise and the patience of Job.''

Dee's heartfelt response made Jenny smile. "I imagine Peter would agree with you,'' she mused. "There are days when I'm so absorbed in my work, the roof could cave in and I wouldn't notice. I lose track of time, forget to eat—''

"I could help you with that," said Dee. "It's not on my resumé, but I took charge of my family's meals as soon as I could reach the sink. If I hadn't, we all would've starved to death."

Jenny laughed and tossed the resumé into the air. "When can you start?"

"How 'bout today?"

"Don't tempt me," Jenny said, then sobering. "Seriously, Dee, it's generous of you to offer, but I couldn't take advantage of you that way."

"But you wouldn't be taking advantage! I love to cook, and I happen to be pretty darn good at it. The Mozart of meat loaf, the Grieg of gravy, the Debussy of dumplings, that's me."

"How are you with pot roast?"

"A poet. One taste is worth a thousand words." Dee touched her fingers to her mouth and threw a kiss toward the ceiling. "Why don't we adjourn to the kitchen? I'll demonstrate."

For Jenny, who had never advanced beyond the shake-and-bake school of cooking, this offer was more than tempting. It was irresistible. "And you say you're not creative," she marveled as she gathered up her crutches. "I should be showing you the office."

"There'll be time for that later," was Dee's no-nonsense reply. She had already regained her composure, and somewhere between the living room and the kitchen her confidence was fully restored.

At the kitchen doorway she paused to survey the layout of the room. She removed her jacket, rolled up her sleeves and nodded approvingly at the utensils that sprouted from earthenware crocks, at the array of copper-bottomed pots and pans that were suspended from their racks within easy reach of the work island. She was on her way to the refrigerator when she spotted the shelf of cookbooks.

"This has to be a put on," she said, regarding Jenny narrowly. "You act as if you can't boil water without scorching it, but the truth is you're a gourmet cook in disguise."

"You're half right," Jenny allowed. "I can boil water without scorching it. Usually. There's been a time or two I've turned on the burner, then forgotten about it till the water boiled away and I wound up ruining the teakettle. I can also make popcorn, scramble eggs and stir up a mean batch of brownies. But aside from that, my culinary skills are limited."

"Sure," said Dee. "That's why you have every small appliance known to man."

"The appliances were gifts from my mother. As far as I'm concerned, they're mostly decorative. You'll notice that the food processor and the pasta machine look brand-new? That's because they've never been used."

"How do you account for the cookbooks?"

"Oh, well, I bought those because I love books, and I can't resist buying them. They're my one extravagance."

"Mine, too." Dee moved in for a closer look at the titles Jenny had collected, and her mood changed yet again. "My God, I don't believe it! You've got *The Settlement Cookbook*." She plucked the volume off the shelf and hugged it to her chest. "My Gram used to swear by this recipe for devil's food cake. And this one, for seven-minute icing. The year I was five, she gave me a birthday party and this was the cake she fixed."

"You can keep the book if you want."

Dee stared at Jenny, agape. "I couldn't."

"Of course you can," Jenny insisted. "I'd like you to have it." After all, to her the book was only a cookbook. To Dee it was a memento of the grandmother she obviously had adored.

A quarter of an hour later, the interview was winding down. While Dee prepared a mysterious blend of spices to season the roast, Jenny sat at the breakfast bar, outlining the responsibilities her assistant would assume.

"One of the difficulties of doing this biography is that Bradley Darien was a diplomat, and since I don't want to rewrite history, I'll need a complete itinerary. I'll have to know where he was, what he was doing and with whom, for every hour of every day, from the time he arrived in Santa Marta."

Dee let out a long, low whistle. "That's a tall order. You're lucky you have eyewitnesses."

"None of them is objective." Jenny slouched over the counter, chin in hand. "Peter...his mother...his Uncle Max. Each of them is biased. Their accounts will be colored by their relationships with Bradley Darien. They'll try to portray him in the most flattering possible light."

"Not consciously," Dee protested.

"No, but it has the same effect. Memories can be very selective. Especially after a loved one's death. It's only human to play down any faults, to suppress recollections that are the least bit negative. And gradually, as the years go by, we remember only the virtues."

"How long ago did Mr. Darien die?"

"About twenty years. That's why it's going to be tough separating fact from fiction."

"However tough it is, you'll pull it off. You did a terrific job on your father's book."

Jenny shrugged off the compliment. "The difference is, I wrote *Diary of a Journalist* within a year of my father's death. Besides, I didn't know him that well."

And as Gareth's only surviving relative, she hadn't had to worry about shattering anyone else's illusions, or stepping on their toes. She hadn't had to worry about her treatment of the subject hurting the man she loved or alienating his family. But she had signed the contract for this book of her own volition, aware of the pitfalls. No one had twisted her arm. No one had coerced her.

Her agreement was an article of good faith. She was honor bound to deliver a manuscript that was as comprehensive, as commercial and as honest as she could make it. She owed that much to Claude LeFevre, her editor at Aldrich and Hayes. And being her father's daughter, she owed it to herself.

"Dad's bio was a cinch compared to this one."

"I'm sure you'll handle it beautifully."

Jenny sighed and sank her chin more deeply into her palm. "I'll have to find corroborating sources of information on events in Santa Marta."

"Mr. Darien's official duties must be a matter of public record."

"Yes, but it's what went on behind the scenes that's most intriguing . . . and probably most dramatic. I'll be relying on you to fill in the gaps."

The moment the words were out, Jenny realized she had spoken as if Dee's coming to work for her was a foregone conclusion. But it wasn't, and part of her urged caution.

What's the rush? said an inner voice. There's no need to hurry. Dee's moody, irrepressible. Sometimes she seems antagonistic. You may be incompatible. At the very least, you ought to talk to Peter about her. Check her references. Don't make a commitment till you've thought it over.

But close on the heels of this advice, another part of her said, Why hesitate? Dee has Peter's recommendation. What more do you want?

Jenny lifted her chin. *Might as well get it over with.* "That's assuming you decide to take the job."

Dee sealed the roast in aluminum foil, and slid it into the oven. "Is that an offer?"

"Yes, it is."

"Then I accept, and for my first assignment I'm going to put your files in order."

As if they're ducks in a row?

Dee's take-charge attitude gave Jenny pause, although her suggestion was not without merit. Collating the notes would acquaint Dee with some of her ideas for Bradley Darien's book, so Jenny didn't argue.

Nor did she take issue with Dee's remark that she couldn't read some of the notes. Jenny knew her handwriting was barely legible. Sometimes even she couldn't decipher it.

As they went through the material, Dee's complaints became more general, but even then Jenny didn't protest.

She didn't draw the line until Dee said, "As long as we're doing this, let's do it right. Let's set up a whole new filing system."

"What's wrong with the system I have?"

Dee held up a sheaf of notes Jenny had grouped together with no discernible logic. "You call this a system?"

"Yes. I call it *my* system."

"But this stuff isn't alphabetized. It's not arranged by date. It doesn't pertain to the same subject. It's so haphazard, I don't see how you can find anything, much less make sense of it."

"Give it time," Jenny said. "It'll be less confusing."

As she told Peter at dinner that evening, "I don't care whether Dee understands my files. What matters is, *I* understand them. If I need information about the rainy season in Santa Marta, or the airport at Playa del Mar, or the annual per-capita income, I know precisely where to find it. At least I did before she got her hands on things."

"If you don't like Dee, why'd you hire her?"

"It's not that I dislike her, but I could do without her nit-picking. Who does she think she is? My mother? The voice of my conscience? Well, I've got news for her. She's not Phyllis, and she's sure as heck no Jiminy Cricket. She's an overbearing, overzealous nag."

"I've noticed she tries too hard," Peter admitted. "I always thought it's because she's anxious to please."

"She's a perfectionist." Jenny glared at Peter, daring him to disagree with her. "Picky, picky, picky. Nothing's good enough to meet her standards."

"Including herself. When you get to know Dee better, you'll realize she's her own worst enemy. She's much more critical of herself than she is with anyone else."

"She deserves it."

"She has a king-size inferiority complex."

"Why should she feel inferior? She has everything going for her, including you to make excuses for her. She's smart, accomplished, *gorgeous*—"

"Hell of a good cook, too." Peter grinned and hefted the serving platter. "More pot roast?"

Jenny declined with a sigh, and his grin vanished.

"Listen, honey, the whole point of hiring an assistant was to take some of the pressure off you. If Dee's not going to make things any easier, why don't you find somebody else?"

"I can't do that. She wanted this job desperately. If I reneged now she'd be terribly disappointed."

"Would you like me to tell her you've changed your mind?"

"No," Jenny answered with an adamant shake of her head. "It's sweet of you to offer, but I got myself into this. I'll get myself out." *Tough it out, more likely.* Unless she could find a way to iron out her differences with Dee.

For the remainder of the evening, Jenny thought of little else.

While Peter read the newspaper, she acknowledged her own culpability.

After an almost sleepless night, she had put in an eight-hour day. By the time Dee arrived her leg ached, she was tired, her frustration threshold was low—in short, she was in no condition to conduct an interview. If she had been, it might have gone very differently.

While Peter took a phone call from his mother, Jenny considered whether she might have misinterpreted some of Dee's comments.

It was possible they were innocent. Maybe she had reacted defensively, when no defense was called for. Maybe she was borrowing trouble. Maybe Dee would become more mellow once she felt secure. And maybe pigs could fly!

"Hold on a minute. I'll ask her." Peter covered the receiver's mouthpiece with his hand and turned to

Jenny. "Mom's spending the weekend at Max's. If you feel up to it, they'd like us to join them."

"There's nothing I'd like better, unless you have other plans."

"Nothing that won't keep." Peter smiled and traced a gentle forefinger along her cheek. "I think it'll do you good to get out."

"So do I," said Jenny.

In fact, the invitation could not have come at a more propitious time. Max Darien's place was in Yolo County, only twenty miles north of Sacramento, yet in some respects it seemed worlds away. The pace was slower there, the air sweeter, and the country breezes were just what she needed to blow away the cobwebs, give her a fresh perspective. . . .

Peter told his mother they'd see her tomorrow and returned to his paper, while Jenny went through the stack of mail that had accumulated on the coffee table the last few days.

There were bills and circulars, a magazine, more bills, a letter from Phyllis, another from Juno Jasperwall, and a nine-by-twelve padded mailer from Aldrich and Hayes.

"Peter, do you remember when this arrived?"

"Nope," he answered. "I'm not sure I've seen it before."

Jenny opened the staples that sealed the envelope and dumped the contents onto the table. A cover letter from Claude LeFevre tumbled out, along with a half dozen smaller envelopes.

Fan mail, she thought, and her spirits rose.

But one of the envelopes had no stamp, no postmark. And on it, her name was misspelled. Only one *n* in Jennifer. No *u* in Spaulding.

Frowning, she slid the envelope toward Peter. "What do you make of this?"

He gave the envelope a cursory glance. "Must be from someone at Aldrich and Hayes."

"But what kind of person takes the time to write a fan letter if he can't be bothered to address it correctly?"

"Obviously not a serious fan."

"Then why bother writing at all?"

After a second look, Peter studied the envelope intently. "What strikes me is that it's printed in block letters. I'll bet it's from a kid."

"There's one way to find out," said Jenny, extracting the note inside.

There was no greeting. No signature. No return address. No date. Only a message cut from newsprint and pasted on a brand of plain white paper commonly sold in variety stores.

hate 1. to have strong dislike or ill will for;—n. a person or thing hated
SYN. *detest* implies vehement dislike or antipathy; *despise* suggests looking down with great contempt upon the person one hates; *abhor* implies a feeling of great repugnance or disgust; *loathe* implies utter abhorrence, and, with persons as the object, connotes the bearing of malice....

Chapter Eight

"What's the verdict?" said Peter. "Is it from a kid?"

"I—I don't think so."

No child could have composed such a message. Only an adult could harbor such intense loathing for someone he—or she?—had never met.

"What does it say?"

Jenny folded the note into its envelope. She moistened her lips with an uneasy flick of her tongue.

"It's a joke. You don't need to see it."

She spoke with all the confidence she could muster, but all the while, she was thinking, *Let it be a joke. Please, God. It has to be a joke.*

If it wasn't, there was nothing she could do about it. At least, nothing practical. Not until Monday. Even then, she wouldn't be able to do much unless, by some miracle, she could find out who'd sent the note.

In the meantime, she resolved not to worry about it. Not to let the message upset her. Not to let it ruin the weekend.

For the next forty-eight hours, she made a diligent effort to keep this vow.

She tried not to think about the note Friday evening, while they watched a movie, or later, when they were lying in bed. Peter took her in his arms and scattered soft kisses across her temples, her forehead, her cheeks. He folded her close and she found forgetfulness in the hard strength of his body... but only for a time.

When she awoke Saturday morning, thoughts of the note were foremost in her mind.

She tried to ignore them while they ate a leisurely breakfast, while they packed overnight bags and drove to Max Darien's place. She tried not to fret that afternoon, while she refereed a tennis match, and that evening, when Lila and she took the best two out of three playing Trivial Pursuit.

But that night, before she turned in, she did find an opportunity to ask Lila if she recalled seeing a nine-by-twelve manila envelope among the mail she'd brought up on Thursday.

"No," Lila answered, "but I don't recall *not* seeing one, either. I really didn't pay that much attention."

Jenny tried not to think about the note on Sunday.

The four of them started the day with brunch at the Nut Tree, and when they got back to Max's house Peter and Max retired to the billiard room, leaving Lila and Jenny to chat.

"There's something I've been wanting to show you," Lila said. Solemnly, with a great show of ceremony, she produced an album of family photos and opened it to a spread of baby pictures.

"Is this Peter?"

"Yes, it is, in all his three-day-old glory. These snapshots were taken the day we brought him home from the hospital."

"Look at him. He's so adorable. So sweet. So... *little*."

"Not *that* little," Lila countered dryly. "As babies go, he was big. His birth weight was eight pounds, twelve ounces." She turned the page. "Here he is at six weeks..."

"At his christening."

Lila nodded. "My grandmother made the dress. In her day, such garments were unisex."

Jenny traced the delicate needlework at the hem of the dress. "This embroidery must've been a labor of love."

"My fondest wish is to see my grandchild wearing it," Lila confided. "What would you guess my chances are of getting my wish?"

"You'd have to ask Peter about that."

"I have asked him. Many times."

"What does he say?"

"He used to put me off, tell me to be patient. When the right girl came along, he'd do what he could to grant my wish. But lately the situation has changed. He's met you, Jennifer." Lila raised a quizzical brow. "Or am I wrong in assuming that I won't have to be patient indefinitely?"

A month ago—even two weeks ago—Jenny would have had a ready answer for Lila's question. Until recently she had felt there was nothing she couldn't share with Peter. No subject was sacrosanct; none was taboo.

Since her accident, however, a reticence had sprung up between them. She sensed there were times when Peter kept his own counsel; she knew there were topics she would rather not discuss. And as she leafed through the album, looking at pictures that recorded Peter's first tooth, his first Christmas, his first birthday, his first steps, Jenny admitted, "We've never talked about children."

If Lila considered this a peculiar oversight, she didn't let on. "I imagine you've given some thought to starting a family, though."

"Oh, yes. I used to dream of having a baby, and once, when I was fifteen or so, I stuffed a pillow under my blouse to see how I'd look if I were pregnant."

Lila laughed. "I wonder if there's an adolescent girl *anywhere* who hasn't done that."

"Probably not, although in my case I'm not sure what inspired it. I hadn't been around children much, except for the summer I was twelve, when I baby-sat for the Ryans, who lived down the block. Florence, their youngest, was born that spring. She was all pink and white and cuddly and soft, and she had this incredible fragrance."

"Talc," said Lila. "Ivory soap. Baby oil—"

"Did Peter smell like that?"

"Most babies do. That and something pure and indefinable."

"Essence of innocence," Jenny suggested. "Eau de new, with a hint of mashed banana."

"Whatever it is, if you could bottle it, you'd make a fortune. But please, Jennifer, go on with your story."

"I was about to say that Florence was at a wonderful age, around three or four months. Young enough to be an infant, old enough to be responsive. Taking care of her was like playing with a real live doll. Her sister Megan, on the other hand, was all scabby knees and perpetual motion. She really kept me hopping. And then there was Timmy. He was a wild and woolly six, with a cowlick and a chocolate mustache and a pocketful of lightning bugs."

"How well I remember," said Lila, rolling her eyes. "What hours did you work?"

"Eight to five-thirty, Monday through Friday."

"More than forty hours a week? That's a tremendous responsibility for a twelve-year-old."

"That's what Phyllis said. She told me I wouldn't last till the end of June."

"Did she really?"

"Yes, but I worked until school resumed that fall."

"Well, you know, it couldn't have been easy for your mother, watching you take your first tentative steps toward independence. She erred, as mothers often do, on the side of being overprotective. But you stuck with it. You didn't allow yourself to be discouraged. When all was said and done, she must have been very proud of you."

"I don't think so. She seemed to feel I'd taken the job to spite her."

"Ah, Jenny! You must be mistaken. Wherever did you get such an idea?"

"I overheard a conversation between Phyllis and Mrs. Ryan. This was during my first week on the job, and I got the impression that Phyllis was checking up on me. Anyway, Mrs. Ryan told her I was 'a regular little mother.' She meant it as a compliment, but Phyllis took it as an insult. I've never seen her so furious."

Even after fifteen years, Jenny could hear the derision in her mother's voice, the outrage in the counterattack she had hurled at Jenny's employer.

"I may not have a fancy sheepskin hanging on my bathroom wall, but I know a put-down when I hear one. And don't bother denying you think you're superior, because I know you do. But the truth is, you're not any smarter or better or more deserving than I am. All you are is lucky. Some of us don't have parents to pave our way. Some of us get pregnant and have to drop out of school, but that doesn't mean we're satisfied to spend the rest of our lives as household drudges. I've pulled myself up by my bootstraps. Everything I have, I've gotten on my own. And my daughter's going to have it easier than I did. Whether she likes it or not, she's going to stay in school. She's going to get her degree. She's going to be a trained professional and have a career. What she's not going to do is fall for the line of some insincere charmer and wind up in a dead-end domestic trap."

Jenny summarized her mother's indictment. She didn't repeat it word for word, although she could have. She would never forget the things Phyllis had said, nor would she forget the devastation, the conflicting rush of emotions she'd felt. The sense of loss and betrayal. The anger. The guilt. The embarrassment. The shame.

She had known all along that her mother resented her. Phyllis had tried to hide it, of course, but children are acutely sensitive to such things. And overhearing that conversation, Jenny had realized how deep the resentment ran; how sharply it was felt.

At age twelve, she had responded in kind. Resentment had bred defiance, which led to increasingly bitter disputes. More than once she'd wanted to scream at her mother, "Don't blame me if you're unhappy. I didn't ask to be born."

In retrospect, Jenny sometimes wondered if she should have screamed at Phyllis. If she had been open about her feelings, it might have cleared the air. They might have been less at odds with each other, more tolerant, more forgiving.

As she told Lila Darien that Sunday, "We might have been friends."

"If you want a reconciliation, I'd advise you to go for it," Lila replied.

"After all these years, I wouldn't know where to begin."

"Where you begin doesn't matter. What's important is that you make the attempt. If there's one thing I've learned in my life, it's that it's never too late to *try*."

THE WEEKEND WOUND to a close. After an early supper, Peter was loading their bags into the car when Lila brought out a box filled with letters, diaries and Bradley Darien's appointment calendars.

"These were my husband's personal papers," she explained. "You might find them useful. The government documents were destroyed when the embassy shut down, and I haven't kept in touch with many of his colleagues, but I went over the personnel roster and wrote in a few updated addresses."

"I'm overwhelmed," Jenny said. "It's awfully nice of you to go to all this trouble. You've saved me a ton of research, and I can't tell you how grateful I am."

"It's my pleasure. Let me know if there's anything else I can do to help."

Before they left Lila added the family album to the box, so that Jenny could refer to it. Jenny thanked her again, and promised to take special care of the pictures and return them as soon as possible.

She took another look at the album that evening, while Peter watched a videotape of the AFC championship game, but it was hard to concentrate with Peter grumbling about penalties and cursing the officials, questioning the acuity of their eyesight and offering crude speculations about their ancestry.

At the end of the first quarter, with the team Peter was rooting for losing ten to nothing and their opponents within striking distance of the goal line, Jenny set aside the album and dug out the nail polish Peter had bought for her.

On the advice of a helpful salesclerk, he'd purchased several bottles. *Persian Melon, Raspberry Sherbet* and *Cranberry.*

She took off the oversize sock that fit over the cast and studied her toes.

They were less swollen, but no more attractive, and so, on the theory that the brightest shade would be most distracting, she tested the cranberry on one toenail.

It was brighter than she had expected . . . the color of a stoplight. Perhaps she should think it over. Or ask Peter's opinion.

She stuffed all three bottles of polish into the pocket of her skirt, grabbed a handful of tissues to wipe up any smears, and returned to the living room, where she found Peter still caught in the grip of play-off fever.

What now? she wondered, eyeing her toes. The painted one stood out like a beacon, but maybe she'd get used to it. *Give it time,* she told herself. And while she came to a decision, she might as well make some popcorn.

She left the polish and tissues on the coffee table, went on to the kitchen, put a packet of popping corn in the microwave, and set the timer. She poured glasses of cold apple cider while she waited for the corn to pop, keeping her ears tuned to Peter's sound effects.

She didn't know much about football, but the way he was groaning told her the opponents had scored again.

Within minutes, the aroma of hot buttered popcorn filled the apartment, and during the next commercial break Peter took a time-out to carry the refreshments into the living room.

Jenny scooped up a handful of popcorn and the bottle of cranberry nail polish, and retired to a corner of the couch.

Peter returned to his game, and while he watched the play-offs, she gauged his team's success from his reactions.

He scowled and winced. He tugged at his hair. He wolfed down popcorn and cider. He pummeled the sofa cushions and drummed his fists against his knees just as Jenny was painting the second toenail. The applicator zigzagged across the tops of her toes, leaving a wake of scarlet polish.

Patting herself on the back for being prepared for this contingency, she set about mopping up the mess.

With the approach of halftime, Peter found something to cheer about when one of the running backs carried the ball deep into enemy territory.

"Yes!" he shouted, jumping to his feet.

Jenny reached for another tissue.

On the next three plays, the team lost ground, but Peter stayed on his feet, pacing the floor as the field-goal unit trotted onto the field.

Jenny used this respite to polish two more nails.

After a long count and a high snap, the kicker booted the ball toward the uprights.

"Yes!" Peter shouted, punching the air as the ball sailed through the air in a tight, arcing spiral.

The trajectory appeared on target. A field goal seemed certain, until the ball suddenly veered to the side and the official signaled the attempt had failed.

The crowd roared, and so did Peter.

"Forty yards! A freakin' chip shot! And he sliced it!"

The network ran the instant replay, and he frowned as if he could change the outcome by sheer force of will.

"The guy's a seasoned veteran. Has the best stats in the league. And he picks this game to choke." Peter heaved a sigh and sank down on the sofa. "I'll say this for him, though. He has plenty of company. The whole offensive line's playing like a bunch of rookies. They get an interception and fumble in the end zone. They block a punt and can't move the ball. Instead of catching up, they're down twenty-four zip."

"They're not beaten yet," Jenny replied. "There's another half to play. Maybe they'll turn things around."

"Yeah, if they don't beat themselves. If they don't have any more turnovers. If they complete a few passes and stop making dumb mistakes. The penalties are killing them!"

Peter might sound disgruntled, but as he leaned back and cradled her feet in his lap, she could feel his tension unraveling.

"Mind the polish. It's not dry yet." She spread her toes, assessing the job she'd done. Now that one foot was finished, the color didn't look half bad. "What do you think? Should I do the rest?"

"One of us should," he said.

Without waiting for her response, he removed her shoe and stocking and held out his hand for the polish. She gave it to him, and held her breath while he painted the nails of the smallest and next smallest toes.

His big sunburned hand dwarfed the applicator, but his touch was sure and his brush strokes were smooth and steady as he painted the third, the fourth, the last toenail.

He bent over her foot, blowing on the polish to dry it, and she lay back against the cushions, content.

"Penalties are a mystery," she said. "Remember when they called pass interference against that player— What d'you call him?"

"Leroy Crawford. The cornerback." Peter shook his head. "That was a costly mistake. Gave 'em first down at the seventeen. Two plays later, they scored."

"And a few plays after that, the same thing happened, except none of the officials saw it."

"They saw it."

"Why didn't they drop their hankies?"

Peter smothered a grin. "Jenny, sweetheart, I don't know how to tell you this, but back in the olden days, before there was such a thing as facial tissues, females used hankies."

"Do tell! And what did men use? Their shirtsleeves?"

"Handkerchiefs. Men used handkerchiefs." He gave her toe a playful pinch, then followed the delicate network of veins to the arch of her foot. "Sometimes, if a girl liked a fella a whole lot, she'd drop her hankie to attract his attention."

"How quaint," said Jenny.

"Also effective. Especially when you consider how repressed Victorians were." His fingers traced a lazy path about her ankle and charted the terrain of her calf. "The hankie could be dropped innocently. It could be dropped casually or serve as a come-on. It could even be an overture to seduction. And if a fella wanted to make his own move, all he had to do was pick up the hankie.''

''I wonder if that's where the term 'pickup' originated?''

''Could be, my little English teacher.''

Peter's hand brushed the hem of her skirt, hesitated for a moment, then coasted beneath the fabric to explore the rise of her knee, the curve of her thigh. And mesmerized by his touch, Jenny lay utterly still.

''But those were simpler times,'' he continued, ''and football's a different game than seduction. It's played in a different arena. On the gridiron, handkerchiefs aren't frilly scraps of linen. They're huge yellow man-size honkers called flags, and they're generally thrown, not dropped.''

She drew in a ragged breath. ''Not in this case.''

''That's because the guy who made the hit was the intended receiver. Since his team had possession of the ball, he had the right to prevent the interception.''

''In other words, all's fair in love and football.''

''Or as we say in the attorney game, possession is nine-tenths of the law.''

His hand roved higher, sending sweet darts of pleasure through her. She saw the excitement in his eyes. She felt the surge of his arousal, and the immediacy of his response made her feel desirable...needed...*cherished*. But some imp of mischief made her reach toward the coffee table and grope for a tissue.

Peter gave her a searching look when it fluttered to the floor. ''Was that dropped or thrown?''

''Thrown,'' she said. ''Definitely thrown. For illegal use of hands.''

''Shall I stop?''

"No! Don't stop!"

"Then what—"

"You'll have to pay the penalty."

"What is it you want me to do?"

Smiling, she opened her arms to him. "Come here, my love. I'll show you."

Chapter Nine

On Monday morning thoughts of the note drew her like a magnet. The moment Peter left for the office, she took another look at it.

On Friday she had focused on the hatred, the loathing. Over the weekend, she had half convinced herself it was the work of a crank. But when she read the note by the clear light of morning, she was struck by the arrogance of the message.

Different words leaped out at her.

Words like *ill will.*

Antipathy.

Contempt.

Malice.

Were they meant to frighten her? To make her question herself and everyone around her? To make her wonder what she had done to provoke such hatred?

Was the note a threat? Did it imply that its author intended to harm her? And if that was the intention, what safeguards could she take? How could she protect herself from a nameless, faceless stranger?

But wait . . .

What if a stranger hadn't sent the note? What if the author was someone she knew? Before she jumped to conclusions, shouldn't she exhaust every possibility?

She glanced at the digital clock on the VCR.

8:36. In New York City it would be 11:36.

With any luck Claude LeFevre should be in his office—if he wasn't in a meeting or off at a conference somewhere.

"Don't be too optimistic," she cautioned herself, as she went to the phone and dialed LeFevre's number. Even if the editor was in, it wasn't likely he'd be able to answer her questions.

But she couldn't help hoping.

While she waited for the call to go through, she rehearsed various ways she might proceed so that her inquiry would seem trivial and workaday—anything to minimize explanations—and when at last Claude came on the line, she wished him a cheery good morning.

"Jenny, this is a delightful surprise! I was just talking about you with Juno Jasperwall. She told me you were injured in some sort of skiing mishap."

"That's a polite way of saying I experienced the agony of defeat on the beginner's hill. I bruised my pride and broke my ankle—"

"My dear, I had no idea! Is there anything I can do? Anything at all?"

"Thanks, Claude, but I think the worst is over. I have a hitch in my giddyup, but I seem to be on the mend now."

"Well, I must say you sound your usual chipper self."

Which proved that Claude was easy to fool, or that she was a better actress than she'd thought.

Jenny glanced at the clock again. 8:47. Dee was due to arrive at nine, so she didn't have much time to bring the conversation around to the note, but she had to observe the niceties. Otherwise Claude might get suspicious. The last thing she wanted was to worry him.

"So," she said brightly, "how's Juno?"

"Superlative, and getting better every minute, to hear her tell it. But you know her, Jennifer. No shortage of ego."

"Or talent."

"Or opinions, for that matter," said LeFevre. "We've been planning the publicity campaign for her new book. She wants the talk-show circuit, a coast-to-coast tour, a full-page ad in *Publishers Weekly*, the whole nine yards."

"Don't we all?"

"Amen! But I say what's the point of going to all that needless expense? She already has enough fans to populate Idaho. So we'll have a few lunches. We'll haggle and bicker and glare at each other over drinks. When all's said and done, for the sake of auld lang syne, we'll compromise."

"And you'll love every minute of it, won't you, Claude?"

LeFevre laughed; he didn't deny it. "Enough about Juno and me. Let's talk about you. Did you receive the batch of fan mail I sent?"

"That's why I called. There's no indication where one of the letters came from, and I wondered if you could tell me where to send my reply."

"Sorry, Jen. I'm afraid I can't. When a letter's addressed to one of our authors, it's treated as personal mail. We accept delivery, but if the author hasn't left other instructions, we don't open it, much less read it or log it in. And because we're functioning as a clearinghouse, most of this correspondence isn't routed through the editorial department."

"Does that include the letters you sent me?"

"Yes, it does. The way they're handled varies from one editor to the next. My standing orders call for the mail clerks to forward my authors' mail either once a month or when there are a half dozen pieces."

"So these letters were actually held in the mail room?"

"Precisely. And when the batch was ready to go, the clerk notified me so that I could send down a cover letter."

8:54. Jenny frowned at the clock. Questioning Claude was a waste of time. Unless— "Is there a chance one of the clerks would have more information?"

"It's possible, I suppose, if there was anything unusual about this particular letter."

"It wasn't sent through the mail," she said. "There was no postage, no postmark. It must have arrived via messenger or come from in-house—"

"Or it may have been enclosed with another piece of mail."

A proposal submitted over-the-transom came to mind. Jenny pictured a landslide of unsolicited manuscripts and sighed, her hopes fading. "I hadn't thought of that," she said.

"Sounds as if this is pretty important to you."

"Important? No, I wouldn't say that, but I'm curious."

"If you'd like, I can check with the clerks—see whether any of them knows anything more about it."

"I know it's a lot to ask, but would you, Claude?"

"As a favor to you? No problem. Give me a few hours. I'll be in touch later today to let you know what I find out."

She thanked LeFevre and hung up the phone just as the numbers on the clock registered nine and, as if on cue, the intercom buzzed.

Evidently, being punctual was another of Dee's virtues.

"You asked for a paragon, you got one," Jenny muttered.

The intercom buzzed again, and she reached for her crutches.

On the way to the door she resolved she would try to be positive.

By summer the book would be written and Dee would be gone. In the meantime, what other option did she have?

Make the best of things, Jenny told herself. *You can do it. If you're determined enough. If you're patient. If you really work at it.*

The buzzer sounded a third time.

She gritted her teeth and amended her vow.

If all else failed, she would think of the pot roast.

DEE WAS FOCUSED. She was efficient. She was prepared. "I wanted to get a feel for your work, so I reread your father's biography—"

"All of it?"

"Most of it." Dee held up the book as if to prove her assertion, but Jenny's dubious gaze made her waver. "Well, a good-size chunk. At least a hundred pages. And do you know what impressed me?"

Jenny thought it might be the cover. Or perhaps the graphics. Or the lack of typos. But in the last-ditch effort to accentuate the positive, she replied with a quiet, "No, what?"

"This book is very compelling," said Dee, riffling the pages. "It's more like an action-adventure novel than nonfiction. So I asked myself why, and the answer I came up with is, your prose style, which is so accessible and straightforward... I might even say linear. It makes the narrative quite easy to read."

Accessible was a critics' term. Jenny had never been sure whether it should be taken as an accolade or the kiss of death. If you weren't accessible, did you need to clarify your work? If you were, was your smog quotient too low? Should you use words with more syllables than flavor? Maybe dig some tongue twisters out of your trusty thesaurus?

Linear she understood perfectly, however. She had always equated this word with logical progression, with inevitability, lucidity and simplicity—the kind of simplicity that did not lack depth or texture; the kind that imbued great art, classical music, epic poetry; the kind of simplicity one associated with grace and elegance and timeless beauty.

But the way Dee said *linear* set Jenny's teeth on edge. Her inflection robbed the word of complexity and the condescending note in her voice gave it a sarcastic twist. She might as well have said *simpleminded.*

Or am I seeing criticism where none is intended? Jenny wondered. Was Dee panning *Diary of a Journalist* or praising it?

"If that was a compliment—"

"It was," said Dee.

"Well, if there's adventure in the book, my father deserves the credit for living an adventurous life."

"You're too modest by far. You're the exception who proves the rule that a biographer has to be scholarly and objective."

Jenny shifted her grip on the crutches and drew herself to her full height. "Bull," she said flatly. "USDA prime."

Dee looked startled. "I take it you don't agree."

"Some rules were made to be broken, especially when it comes to writing. If everyone stuck to the rules, there wouldn't be anything worth reading. Fiction would be formulaic. Nonfiction would be dry and boring. As for biography, tell me how I can do justice to my subject if I remain distant, if I don't invest something of myself in a book. Heart...soul...compassion...imagination... Call it what you will. If I can't put myself in my subject's place—see things as he sees them, feel his joy, feel his pain—how can his story be anything more than a bloodless collection of facts?"

Dee responded to Jenny's disquisition with vigorous bobs of her head. "Yes," she said, nodding thoughtfully. "Yes, of course. I see your point and I couldn't agree with you more." But there was no understanding in her eyes.

Before she could recover, Jenny announced that she was going to get started on her outline. She headed for the office, with Dee hot on her heels.

"Would you like me to bring you some coffee?"

"No. Help yourself if you like, but I don't want to be disturbed."

Dee trotted ahead to open the office door. "What would you like me to do?"

Jenny glanced toward the living room, over her shoulder. "There's a boxful of papers on the sofa. You can sort through those."

"That won't take more than an hour...maybe two. What should I do when I'm done?"

"Go to the library. Read whatever you can find about the climate in Santa Marta." *Anything* to get rid of the woman.

Jenny eased into her swivel chair and propped the crutches nearby. She booted up the computer, wondering how she could manage to concentrate with Dee hovering over her, watching her like a hawk.

The CRT came to life amidst a chorus of mechanical hums and chirps. Amber letters flashed across the screen as the circuitry took stock of its condition and gave her the all clear. She removed the DOS disk and inserted the program and data disks. More hums. More letters. More chirps. And finally the prompts.

Jenny cued up a document while Dee looked on.

"I'll have to learn to use your program," she said.

"You can borrow the manuals. Take them home with you."

"I thought maybe you wouldn't mind if I watched for a while."

"Not today." Nor in this lifetime, Jenny thought. "There's one thing you can do for me." she said.

Dee leaned forward, anxious to be of service.

"Close the door on your way out."

ALONE, SHE STARED at the terminal screen and suffered pangs of conscience.

The screen stared back. Its winking cursor seemed to accuse her—of what?

Being a grouch?

Being paranoid?

Making mountains out of molehills?

Jenny chewed absently at her lower lip as she considered her aversion to Delores Chapin. It could be a side effect of her injury, of the more or less constant discomfort that reminded her she was not at her best.

Aside from a faux pas or two, what had Dee said that was so terrible? What awful things had she done? She seemed knowledgeable, hardworking, willing to learn, eager to please. . . .

Is she too willing? Too eager? Is that why I don't trust her?

Jenny rolled her chair away from the terminal and spun toward the window, admitting the possibility that she would be suspicious of any stranger who came into her life just now. In light of Toni's prediction, this was not an unreasonable reaction.

And then there was the note.

Dee could have slipped it into the envelope last Friday, when they were going through the files. She'd had plenty of opportunities. But so had the men who delivered the bed.

It might have been prudent to fire Dee, but if she hadn't sent the note, it wouldn't be fair to let her go, and if she had sent the note, it seemed the lesser of two evils to keep her on and find out what she was up to. Give her enough rope to hang herself.

"I'll be darned if I'll apologize," Jenny murmured, wheeling back to the terminal

Given the choice between running scared and being angry, she would rather be angry any old time, even if anger was uncalled for.

DEE TURNED OUT TO BE a competent watchdog. There were several phone calls that morning, which she handled without bothering Jenny.

At about ten-thirty the intercom buzzed. Dee took care of that, as well. A minute later, Jenny heard muffled voices in the entryway, then footsteps crossing the living room and a knock at the office door.

"Sorry to interrupt," Dee called, "but there's a man here with some fish."

"It's okay," Jenny said. "We were expecting them."

Shortly after eleven Dee knocked at the door again to let Jenny know she had finished sorting the papers. "The files are in the box, your messages are by the phone and the fish are in the aquarium. The man left instructions and a schedule of days he'll stop by to take care of them. That's by the telephone, too. Oh, and I made myself some coffee. There's half a pot left. Do you want me to leave the warming tray on or turn it off?"

"Leave it on," Jenny said.

"If there's nothing else you'd like me to do before I leave, I'm on my way to the library."

"Don't forget to keep track of your hours."

"I won't," came the answer. "See you Wednesday."

Dee had scarcely left when there was a knock at the front door. This time the caller was Rita. Jenny's welcome was less than gracious.

"You're not at work."

"And you're not much of a hostess. Aren't you going to invite me in?"

Jenny stood her ground, squarely on the threshold. "Actually, Rita, this isn't a good time. I'm up to my ears—"

"In an outline. I know. I ran into Betty Coed downstairs, and she told me you're in your creative mode, but there's something I wanted to talk to you about—"

"I'm listening," said Jenny.

"Not here in the hall, for God's sake. This is personal. It's private!"

"Then I'd advise you to keep it to yourself." Jenny made a move to close the door; Rita poked one foot in to prop it open.

"It concerns you," she said. "I figured you'd want to hear it."

Jenny gave Rita an incredulous stare, debating whether it would be quicker to let her in or keep her out?

"Don't you bestselling author types take a break now and then? Hell! Even nurses get their days off."

In, Jenny realized. Most emphatically *in.* "Before you come in, let's get one thing straight. On days when I'm writing, my breaks are never longer than fifteen minutes."

"What happens if I stay twenty?"

"You'll wear out your welcome, and I'll lock myself in my office."

"Gee, I was kinda hoping you'd turn into a pumpkin."

Grinning, Rita sauntered into the living room. Jenny was about to follow when Bev Rudolph sailed into view, her face pink with exertion. "Is my roommate here?"

Jenny opened the door wider. "Come on in. Everyone else has." With so many people wandering through, one more couldn't make any difference.

She moved aside with an airy wave toward the living room, and stayed in the entryway while Bev scurried by and caught up with Rita.

"There you are," Bev scolded in a harsh nagging tone. "I've been looking all over for you. You have a phone call. He says it's urgent."

"He who?"

"How should I know? He wouldn't leave his name. My guess is, he's one of your playmates and probably married."

"So big deal," Rita complained as she and Bev marched out. "What if he *is* married? What are you? My conscience?"

"Come again when you can stay longer." Jenny mouthed the pleasantry toward their swiftly retreating backs. She waited till they clattered downstairs, into their own apartment, then closed the door firmly, turned the dead bolt and slid the security chain onto its track.

No more Grand Central Station. From now on, she would keep the door chained.

CLAUDE LEFEVRE WAS as good as his word. At a few minutes past one, he phoned to let Jenny know that the mail clerks knew nothing about the note.

"Do you find that surprising?" she asked.

"No," said LeFevre. "You wouldn't either, if you had any idea how high the turnover is down in the mail room. Most of these folks are temporaries. For what it's worth, though, a couple of the old-timers said they would have remembered your letter if they'd seen it, and neither of them seemed to think it could have originated in-house."

What do I do now? Jenny wondered. She'd known all along that Claude's inquiry was a long shot; still, she was disappointed that he'd learned so little.

Apparently Claude sensed how she felt. "Listen, Jen, I'm not sure what's going on, but if there's any way I can be of assistance, just say the word."

"Thanks anyway, Claude. I'll take it from here."

His offer made it clear that she would have to help herself. There was nothing more he could do. Absolutely nothing. But she wasn't beaten yet. There was another avenue she could explore.

AT ONE-THIRTY that afternoon, keeping a wary eye on Rita's door, Jenny made her way downstairs to the vestibule. After a twenty-minute wait, the postal-service truck pulled into the drive.

Jenny had always prided herself on being observant. As a writer, this was one of the tools of her trade, but as the mail carrier climbed out of the van it occurred to Jenny that, although they had talked before, she had never looked at the mail carrier closely enough to see beyond the unflattering blue gray uniform.

But as Jenny watched her swing the bulky pouch over her shoulder, she registered details of the mail carrier's appearance, and saw a woman of medium height, medium build, who was neither homely nor beautiful.

Everything about her struck Jenny as average, aside from her gingery hair, which reminded Jenny of Betty Holtz, and a certain athletic ability, made evident from the ease with which she handled the heavy bag.

Despite its weight, she breezed into the lobby with a light, springy stride, and when she spotted Jenny lurking in the corner, the puckish smile that spread across her freckled face was as carefree as her spirit.

"Hi-dee-ho," she said in a lazy drawl. "How's every little thing goin'?"

"Not bad," Jenny answered.

"Not good either, from the looks of you." The mail carrier summed up her appearance with a glance, as she unlocked the bank of mailboxes. "If you don't mind my sayin' so, you look a mite peaked."

"Peaked . . . Yes," Jenny agreed numbly.

Until that moment, she hadn't realized how dependent she had become upon other people's flattery. Somewhat shaken, she watched the carrier move from box to box, depositing the day's mail.

"This is embarrassin'. I shouldn't have spoke out of turn."

"But you're right," Jenny said. "I do look peaked. I can't say the truth doesn't hurt, but it's a relief to hear it. I guess it's the sort of thing even your best friend won't tell you."

"Well, aren't you nice, takin' it that way!"

The mail carrier turned to hand Jenny her mail, and Jenny caught a glimpse of the plastic name tag pinned to her blouse. *R. Pierson,* it said.

"Look, Miss Pierson—"

"Call me Raette."

Jenny fought back a giggle, but she couldn't help smiling. "That's what the *R* stands for?"

"Yes'm, and if you feel inclined to laugh, go ahead. Won't hurt my feelings a'tall. Raette was my momma's notion of fancy, but it's the cross I carry, going through life with a given name that reminds most folks of one of those new synthetics."

"Or a hair spray," said Jenny.

"Or one of those fazers they use on *Star Trek,*" Raette finished. "So Miss Spaulding—"

"My name's Jenny."

"Okey-doke, Jenny. Now that I've made your day, is there anything else I can do for you?"

"I hope so," she replied. "I received a parcel last week from New York City. It was a nine-by-twelve padded mailer, about so thick . . ." She measured half an inch or so between her thumb and forefinger. "I wondered if you might remember it?"

"Sounds like the one I delivered on Wednesday."

"Do you recall how it was sealed? Was it stapled or taped?"

"Why? Was there something wrong with it?"

"It may have been tampered with."

"Aw, shoot! I knew I shouldn't have left it."

"You *left* it?"

"Sure 'nough. Right here, on top of the mailboxes. It wouldn't fit inside." Raette lowered the metal housing that covered the boxes and locked it. "Many's the time I've done it before, with nary a problem. There's never been any pilferage in this building, and the tenants like the convenience. But this time—I don't know—I had a funny feelin' I should stick to regulations. I was about to leave an 'attempt to deliver' notice in your box—"

"What changed your mind?"

"I remembered you were laid up, and I thought you'd take it kindly if I saved you a trip to the post office."

"Why didn't you bring the parcel upstairs, to my apartment?"

"I buzzed," said Raette. "Nobody answered."

"But I was home!" Jenny protested. Then, recalling her afternoon naps, "I must've been sleeping."

"Well, I guess that's my bad luck, but like the Bible says, 'As ye sow, so shall ye reap.' It all evens out in the end." Raette shrugged philosophically. "Truth is, I don't recollect how that parcel was sealed, but there's one thing I can tell you. If you think your mail was tampered with, you ought to fill out a complaint."

"What will happen if I do?"

"The postal service has inspectors. I've heard tell they're real bloodhounds. They'd check this whole deal out, recover whatever was stolen and prob'ly find out who took it."

"And what would happen to you?"

"Nothin' I can't handle." All business now, Raette slung the mail pouch over her shoulder. "The forms are in my van. If you'll hang on a minute, I'll get you one."

"That won't be necessary. I'd rather not file a complaint."

Raette hesitated, one hand on the door. "Before you make up your mind, there's something I oughta tell you."

"I'm listening," said Jenny.

"The real reason I wanted to do you a good turn didn't have much to do with those crutches."

"Then why—"

"I've been workin' up the courage to ask you to sign your books."

"You don't need courage for that," Jenny replied. "I take it as a compliment when readers ask for my autograph."

"Then you wouldn't mind if I brought my copies by some day?"

Jenny shook her head. "I'm curious about one thing, though. If I weren't a writer, would it have made any difference in the way you handled the parcel?"

"None whatever. It's just I didn't want to leave you with the wrong impression."

"Thanks," said Jenny. "I appreciate that."

"One more thing, and I'll be on my way. From now on, you can bet your bottom dollar I'll go by the book, *strictly* by the book."

"In that case, Raette, I don't see that there's anything to gain from filing a complaint."

Jenny saw the look of gratitude on Raette's face. She saw the jaunty way Raette climbed into the van, and as the mail truck disappeared along the drive, she knew that she'd made the right decision.

Yes, the package of fan mail had been left unattended for several hours. Anyone passing through the lobby could have opened it, put in the anonymous letter and sealed the mailer with staples.

But there was nothing to corroborate this sequence of events. There was no proof her mail had been tampered with, and without proof the idea of an official investigation seemed premature and slightly preposterous.

An investigation wouldn't accomplish a thing, except to stir up trouble for Raette. She might get a reprimand, lose a promotion. She might even lose her job.

And all, Jenny realized, because she tried to do me a favor.

Jenny put the day's mail in the pocket of her sweater and started across the vestibule toward the stairs, recalling another place, another time, when a poison-pen letter had exacted its price from her.

She had lost friendships, her reputation, her teaching position, her peace of mind....

But the most insidious thing about it was, she'd felt partially responsible. She'd blamed herself. She'd been more than a little convinced that she must have done something to provoke the attack.

All of which had played into her tormentor's hands.

And to make matters worse, she had compounded her predicament by running scared.

She had *let* herself be victimized, but never again. She'd learned from her mistakes. She was not about to repeat them.

This time she wouldn't allow the letter to work its poison. She wouldn't let the creep who'd written it orchestrate her behavior. She wouldn't panic, and she certainly wouldn't hold herself responsible.

"I'll fight back," she declared, as she mounted the stairs.

Instead of reacting with fear and secrecy, she'd do what she should have done in the first place. She would show the note to Peter.

She stopped for a moment, imagining his response.

Initially he would be outraged. Indignant. Upset. There was a good chance he'd be angry with her. He'd want to know why she hadn't told him about the note immediately, and she would tell him she'd felt ashamed, that being the target of animosity—of hate mail—made her feel as if, somehow, she deserved it.

Peter would understand, of course, even though he'd be hurt that she had any misgivings about taking him into her confidence. He would say, "I thought you trusted me." And she would say, "I do trust you, Peter. That's why I'm showing you the note now. I didn't want there to be any obstacles between us."

He would know she was telling the truth and he would take her in his arms and comfort her. "Don't worry about the note," he'd say. "I'll get to the bottom of it."

Peter would hold her close and safe. She would promise never to doubt him again, and he would promise he'd always be there to protect her.

"Not that you can't take care of yourself," he would say, "but sometimes it's nice to have someone to lean on."

Perhaps he would tease her because she'd been so silly. She would laugh, and he'd laugh with her. They would pledge there would be no more secrets....

Jenny negotiated the last of the stairs and covered the distance to her apartment, consoled by the thought that something positive might come from the note. Something of infinite value.

Once in the entry hall she paused to chain the door, then headed for the living room.

The padded mailer was on the lamp table, where she'd left it. It didn't appear to have been touched since she'd put it there that morning, but when she looked through the letters, she discovered one was missing.

She peered into the mailer and found it empty. Frowning with disbelief, she looked through the letters again and yet again before she was willing to acknowledge she had not been mistaken.

The anonymous note was gone.

Chapter Ten

"That does it. Enough is enough."

Jenny's voice shook with annoyance. She headed for the office and fumbled through the Rolodex with hands that were none too steady. She found Rita's number and punched it into the phone with irate jabs of her forefinger. Her response to Rita's "Hello" was a curt, "Where is it?"

"Excuse me? I don't—"

"Drop the act, Rita. Just tell me where it is."

"Jenny? What in the— Is this some kind of joke?"

"Not to me, it isn't. If you think I'm going to let you get away with taking the letter, you're—"

"What letter?"

"You know perfectly well what letter."

"I don't, Jenny. Scout's honor. But if you'll calm down and tell me what this is all about, I'll do what I can to help."

Jenny could feel her temper rising to a boil, threatening to erupt any second. "I don't want to calm down. I don't want your help. I don't want to play your stupid game any more. When you kept my pen I didn't say much because it could have been an honest mistake. When you took the magnet and the shell and the soaps,

I didn't make waves because you're a neighbor, but tampering with the mail is a federal offense."

"You've got a nerve, accusing me—"

"This is not an accusation. It's a warning. Either you bring back my letter or I'll press charges. I swear I will! This time you've gone too far. I'm fed up. I've had it!"

"That makes two of us," Rita answered. "I thought you were my friend, Jenny Spaulding, but obviously I was wrong. You're too selfish to be anyone's friend. You're so uptight about losing a few knickknacks, it's pathetic. You can't see what's going on under your own sorry nose."

"Maybe not, but I know when someone's trying to pull the wool over my eyes!"

"You got that right, but I'll bet you don't know who."

Jenny's grip on the receiver tightened. "Listen, Rita—"

"No, *you* listen. I don't know diddly about this letter of yours, but someone *is* trying to fool you. *Two* someones, in fact. Peter and whozits...your new assistant."

"Dee," Jenny supplied the name automatically, numbly, uncertain where this was leading. "Dee Chapin."

"Whatever. Last Friday, when I came home from work, Peter's car was parked out front. I wondered why he'd park on the street instead of pulling into the garage, so I took a little stroll to the end of the drive, and that's when I noticed he was sitting in the car. He seemed to be waiting for someone, only the way he was slouched down in the driver's seat made me think it wasn't you. Needless to say, I found that extremely curious, so I hid behind the hedge. About ten minutes later, who should come out of the building but Dee. She got in the car with Peter and off they went."

"Sorry to disappoint you, but there's a simple explanation." *There has to be,* Jenny thought, praying for inspiration. *Why hadn't Peter mentioned the incident?* She inhaled deeply and continued with an air of false confidence. "Peter recommended Dee for the job. He must have stopped by to find out how the interview went, and since he happened to be here when she was leaving, he gave her a ride home. There's nothing underhanded about that."

"Not on the surface," Rita agreed. "God knows I wouldn't have given it another thought if they hadn't looked so cozy together, and so excited and . . . Well, frankly, it was as if they get their kicks out of sneaking, if you know what I mean. Then, too, Peter was waiting for her again today, different time, same station."

"Coincidence," said Jenny. She refused to believe there was anything more to it than that.

Rita's hoot of laughter said that she shouldn't dismiss it so lightly. "You're living in a dream world. Once could be a coincidence. I'll give you that. But twice? No way!"

"That's your interpretation."

"It's reality, and here's what gives it away. The minute Dee set foot in the car, Peter took off. Now, I ask you, why would he park in the street and make such a fast getaway if he didn't have something to hide? It's not as if either of them was in a tearing hurry to get to lunch."

"I repeat," said Jenny, "that's your interpretation. Or perhaps I should say *mis*interpretation. Considering the source, I see no cause for alarm."

"Are you calling me a liar?"

"You're a gossip, Rita. You have a talent for seeing the worst in everybody."

"My talent is honesty," Rita declared.

"Oh, right. I'd forgotten. You're the one with no axes to grind, no tricks up her sleeve. The one who doesn't sugarcoat the truth. The one who cannot tell a lie."

"Not knowingly," Rita replied with saccharine sweetness. "And here's an unadulterated truth for you, kiddo. You ought to take off those rose-colored glasses before it's too late. Or are they off already? Are you only pretending? You don't have to, you know. Not with me. I know how much you care for Peter, and in spite of your low opinion of me, I consider you a friend. Believe me, it's no fun being the bearer of bad tidings."

"Then why are you telling me these things?"

"Somebody has to. You need to know them for your own good."

"Do you expect me to believe that?"

Rita sighed with exasperation. "What is it with you? Are you some sort of masochist? Don't you mind sharing your boyfriend with Betty Coed?"

"What I am is steamed, Rita. That's the last straw."

On that exit line, Jenny hung up the phone. She wished it were as easy to disconnect her thoughts.

Not that she took Rita's charges seriously. Peter loved her! She knew he did. How could she doubt his passion after the way he'd made love to her last night?

How could she doubt the depth of his feelings when he proved them day by day in the myriad thoughtful things he did to make her recuperation easier?

How could she doubt his sincerity, when she had proof of it on her cast, in the proposal he'd written, in the heart he had drawn?

But it wasn't Peter's love she questioned, or his passion, or his sincerity. What she doubted was her own appeal.

Her appearance seemed to diminish every time she looked in the mirror. Which was why she'd developed an aversion to mirrors lately, especially brightly lighted bathroom mirrors. It was also why, when the light bulbs burned out in the bedroom, she was in no hurry to replace them.

These days, like Peter's new headboard, she was at her best in the dark. And Peter must have noticed. After all, he was only human.

He was also a vigorous, virile, lusty man with a robust libido and a healthy interest in the opposite sex. And being human, and being a man, he could be tempted. He might even become infatuated, and then...

"No!" Jenny cried.

She loved Peter. She trusted him. She knew she could rely on his integrity. Why was she torturing herself with thoughts of his becoming romantically involved with Dee?

The idea was too painful to contemplate, yet it haunted her. She couldn't put it out of her mind.

Getting out of the apartment might have broken the cycle. A few weeks ago she would have gone for a drive, maybe taken a walk. But now that she had to contend with the cast, she didn't have these options.

The walls of the living room seemed to close in on her as she glanced through her phone messages and read the day's mail. There was a message on the answering machine, and she rewound the tape and played it back.

"Jenny, this is Dee. It's a little after one-forty-five and I'm phoning from the library. Somehow or other a letter of yours got mixed in with my notes and I picked it up by mistake. I wanted to apologize for the mix-up and let you know I'll bring it back Wednesday. If you need it before then, give me a call. You can reach me here till six or so. After that, I'll be at home. See ya."

"Talk about mix-ups," Jenny muttered.

If she hadn't gone downstairs to wait for the mail carrier, she would have been here to take Dee's call. And if she'd taken the call, she wouldn't have assumed Rita had taken the letter. She wouldn't have accused Rita, and Rita wouldn't have felt obliged to retaliate by—

No. That wasn't quite right. Rita relished spreading gossip. She had paid a special visit earlier today to talk about something "personal." Something "private." And whatever her motivation, Rita was not responsible for Peter's indiscretions. *If* he had been indiscreet.

I suppose I owe her an apology, Jenny thought. For jumping to conclusions. For blaming her.

But Jenny didn't feel apologetic and she didn't want to talk to Rita.

She poured a cup of coffee and drank it, sitting at the kitchen counter. It was from the pot Dee had made that morning, and after standing for hours on the warming tray it tasted as black and bitter as her mood.

Even when she returned to the computer and tried to work, her treacherous memory wouldn't stop dredging up snippets of her conversation with Rita.

They looked so cozy together, Rita had said. *And excited. As if they get their kicks out of sneaking.*

Take off those rose-colored glasses, she'd said. *Before it's too late.*

Three o'clock came and went. Four o'clock. Five.

Afternoon faded to evening and still Jenny couldn't shake the feeling that, somewhere among Rita's insinuations, there must be an element of truth.

If there was nothing personal between Peter and Dee, if their meetings weren't assignations, if they were accidents, completely innocent, why hadn't he mentioned them?

Why would he act as if he were hiding something if he didn't have something to hide?

If Jenny asked, how would he respond?

Did she want to know the answers? Did she want to know them *tonight?* If they weren't to her liking, how could she bear the unbearable?

A showdown was inevitable, but it could be postponed. A day or two might make a difference. Three days might make it easier to cope.

A week would be even better. Circumstances could change drastically in a week. Miracles could happen. A universe could be created. An infatuation could burn itself out....

Jenny switched on a lamp and flipped through the pages of her desk calendar, scanning the daily reminders.

Her appointment with the orthopedist was a week from Wednesday; the nurse had promised her a walking cast. She would have more mobility then. She could come and go as she pleased, and she would be stronger, more herself. The only question was, could she play ostrich that long?

"Who do you think you're kidding?" she muttered, and without stopping to weigh the consequences, reached for a marking pen and circled the date with Day-Glo red.

She had always believed that knowledge was power—until this afternoon. Since the phone call to Rita, she had discovered it wasn't necessarily so.

And as she sat in her office that evening, waiting for Peter to come home, Jenny studied the calendar. She recognized the incriminating wobbles in the circle as places where her hand had faltered, and made another discovery.

There were times when knowledge was power; others when knowledge was fear. And then there were times like this, when ignorance was bliss.

"You've colored your hair," Dr. Everett said.

"I'm giving it some thought."

She raised one hand to the feathery bob, separated a strand and pulled it forward to assess the color. In the restful light of the psychiatrist's office it was not quite sherry brown, but a close enough match as makes no difference. A shade or two darker than Jenny's, at most.

Satisfied, she finger-combed the strand into place, smiling at Everett's baffled expression.

"This is a wig I'm trying out," she said. "If I decide it suits me, I'll make the switch, and only my hairdresser will know for sure."

The analyst was visibly relieved. For a moment, she thought he might break down and smile. "I'll know. So will you."

"But I'll never tell, and you don't count. You took an oath that says you've gotta keep my secrets, didn't you, Dr. Everett?" She lifted the hair away from her collar and fluffed the bangs with a toss of her head. "What do you think? Is it me?"

"You realize I'm no fashion expert."

How could she not? One look at his tie and baggy tweeds told her he'd never make the best-dressed list. But she gave him a sidelong glance from beneath her lashes, as if she hadn't noticed his wardrobe, and persisted in a throaty, flirtatious voice that invited compliments.

"I'd appreciate it if you'd tell me your reaction as a man."

"As a man I'd have to ask what's wrong with your natural color?"

"Nothing. I just felt like a change. You know what they say. Variety's the spice. Besides, it's been so long since I've seen my natural color, for all I know this might be it."

Everett rocked back in his chair and puffed on his pipe. The silence between them became as dense as the smoke.

"So how about the wig?" she prompted. "Do you like it?"

"Yes, I think it's very attractive, although it does seem a trifle subdued for you."

Drab was more like it, she thought. But she felt a jolt of triumph. Not only had she maneuvered the psychiatrist into a corner and forced him to express his opinion; he had also paid her a compliment.

"The style's not right for me." She pulled the hair away from her face, sucked in her cheeks, then fluffed the hair back into place. "It's too full around the temples. It makes my face look fat. And I'd have to redo my makeup—"

Everett cut her off with a nod. "I'd like to go back to your comment about variety being the spice. It brings to mind another saying. 'Imitation is the sincerest form of flattery.' I wonder if you're familiar with it?"

"It rings a bell, but you're way out in left field if you think I'm imitating anyone."

"What about Celia? If I were a betting man, I'd wager her hair was the same color as yours."

She stared at the analyst, startled by his brusque change of subject and more than a little uneasy. Was his comment a fishing expedition or a lucky guess? If he wasn't guessing, what else did he know? How much did he suspect?

"You may be right, Dr. Everett. I don't exactly remember the color of Celia's hair."

"You don't have any photographs of her?"

"They were destroyed in the fire."

"Of course. I should have thought of that. But still, I'm surprised by an odd inconsistency."

"Inconsistency?"

"Yes. You seem to recall her husband vividly, while your recollections of her are sketchy. Yet you maintain the two of you were inseparable."

"We were this close." She held up crossed fingers. "Like sisters."

"So you've said, and that makes your selective amnesia even more intriguing." Everett rested his head against the back of his chair and blew twin streamers of smoke toward the ceiling.

Here it comes, she realized. Another sermon.

"Repression is a relief valve that protects the psyche. It's a mechanism commonly seen in patients with post-traumatic stress disorder..."

She wanted to scream at Everett, tell him to shut up. Big shot analyst. Full of crap. Cranking out platitudes like sausages. He considered himself an authority, but what did he know about trauma or stress? What did he know about anything?

For two cents she'd tell him a few hard facts. She could tell him what it was like to want something so much you could taste it, so much that the wanting became a physical ache, so much that you'd do whatever it took to possess it, so much that you'd lie, cheat, steal... even kill if you had to.

She could tell Everett what it was like to have the very thing you desired within your grasp, only to have someone less deserving snatch it away.

She could tell him about envy, about jealousy, about hatred. If she really wanted to shock him, she could tell him the truth about Celia. It might be worth it to see the horror on his face.

"...It follows that your memory would erase the tragic circumstances surrounding your friend's death, but what's uncommon about your case..."

Not yet, she thought. It was much too soon for open defiance. She didn't want to tip her hand. But in another month or two, she'd be ready to make her move, and then, who knew what might happen. As Everett droned on, the voice of reason prevailed. She held her tongue and masked her resentment.

Let him talk, she told herself. I don't have to listen.

One, one thousand... two, one thousand... On the count of eighty-eight, she tuned him back in.

"...Now you claim you've forgotten the color of Celia's hair. You'll have to pardon me if I find that incredible."

So he didn't believe her. She'd known that all along. But he'd never said it before in so many words.

"Has it occurred to you that I may not want to remember?"

"It might be more to the point if I were to ask you that question," Everett replied. He sat quietly for a full

minute, as if to let his answer sink in, then gave her a verbal pat on the head. "The fact that you've raised the issue shows a degree of insight."

"That's good, isn't it?"

"It's a step forward, certainly. However, if we are to progress any further, you'll have to work through your memory lapses."

"How, Doctor? How can I do that?"

"I think we should try hypnosis."

Hypnosis! *Damn control freak. She might have known he'd prescribe a course of treatment that put her in an impossible situation. If she agreed to the suggestion, she risked exposure. If she didn't agree, he'd report her lack of cooperation to the warden and she'd land in jail. All her plans would come to nothing. Everything she'd worked for would go down the drain. Unless she could play for time.*

"You know I'll do whatever you recommend. But hypnosis?" *She hugged her arms, faking a shudder.* "It's kind of scary."

"There's no reason to be frightened. It's perfectly safe."

"What if I go into a trance and don't come out?"

"I assure you, that would never happen."

She sneaked a peek at her watch. The hour was almost up. She averted her gaze and slumped forward, so that the hunched curve of her shoulders conveyed dejection. "Could I have some time to get used to the idea?"

"I see no reason why not."

She caught the tender lining inside her cheek between her teeth and clamped down hard, bruising her mouth. She tasted blood. The pain made her eyes water, and when she raised her eyes the tears spilled over.

It was a trick she'd learned ages ago, and she did it well. It was hammy, but effective. Everett was sufficiently moved to offer her a handful of tissues and a stay of sentence.

"If it would help put your mind at rest, I have some pamphlets on hypnosis you can read."

She pressed the tissues to her eyes and answered between sniffles, "Thank you, Doctor. I'm very grateful."

Everett rose, signaling the end of the session. She left his office weighed down by the pamphlets. But once the door closed behind her, she headed for the elevator with a lighthearted spring in her step.

She had dodged a bullet today. No two ways about that. And if she had to, she'd dodge it again.

She felt invincible.

She felt like celebrating, because this time around she would get what she wanted. She'd let no one stand in her way. Not the warden. Not the shrink. Not Jenny Spaulding.

When the elevator came, she stepped into the crowded car humming beneath her breath. The other passengers exchanged glances and smiles.

"'Light My Fire,'" she proclaimed to no one in particular as the car glided to a stop on the street floor. "If it was good enough for Jim Morrison, it's good enough for me."

Chapter Eleven

Jenny found herself marking time, not always gracefully. There were moments when she was utterly convinced that Rita's allegations were unfounded. Peter loved her more than ever. He would never be unfaithful. Dee was a gem, and if occasionally something she said or did struck a sour note, it wasn't her fault. Jenny was hypersensitive. She was oversuspicious. She was jumping to conclusions as she had with the letter.

Betty Holtz summed up her problem nicely when they talked on the phone on Tuesday. "You start off with a preconceived notion, and if you look for something to support it hard enough, long enough, sooner or later you're bound to find it."

Jenny recognized the wisdom in her friend's advice. She promised Betty it would be her watchword, but a smile, a look, a chance comment could shatter her resolve.

The certainty that Peter was keeping something from her made her more watchful, but he seemed as watchful as she.

On Thursday, she was putting the finishing touches on her outline when he left a message with Dee. "He won't be home for dinner. He has some sort of conference tonight."

"Why didn't you tell me he was on the phone?" Jenny demanded.

"You said you didn't want to be disturbed."

"That doesn't include Peter."

"Whatever you say, boss. Me Indian, you chief."

Dee's reply rankled. So did her good-natured shrug. She was on her way out the door when Jenny inquired, "Didn't he ask to speak to me?"

"Nope. Poor guy was too busy, I guess."

Poor guy, indeed! Jenny fumed. Too busy to talk to me, but not too busy to spend the better part of fifteen minutes on the phone with Dee! She'd overheard Dee's end of the conversation. Parts of it, anyway. Enough giggling and whispering to make her wish she'd paid more attention. Enough to leave her feeling totally demoralized.

That night when Peter got home she was in the bedroom, watching the stately silver-and-black angelfish play follow-the-leader through the swaying fronds of the anemones. In the corner of the tank closest to the aerator, white polka-dotted percolas swam up and down in a splash of fiery orange. They were show-offs, the clowns of the aquarium, and after each up-and-down circuit the one she'd named Emmett, in honor of Emmett Kelly, floated to the surface and looked out at her with a fixed fishy stare.

She knew that he was begging for a pinch of fish food, but she was too apathetic to give him his reward, just as she hadn't the heart to say anything when Peter came in. Instead of calling out, "Hi, sweetheart. How was your day?" she listened to the telltale sounds that told her Peter was in the kitchen, foraging through the refrigerator for something to drink.

She heard ice rattling against a glass as he wandered back into the living room, and then the TV came on. Although he kept the volume tuned low, she recognized the voice of one of the sports reporters on CNN.

But still she didn't say anything until a few minutes later, when Peter turned the TV off and came into the darkened bedroom.

The light from the aquarium allowed him to see that she was awake. It allowed her to see that he was carrying his shoes in one hand; with two fingers of the other hand he had hooked his sport coat over his shoulder. His hair was rumpled and he looked a bit bleary-eyed.

Maybe he actually was working, she thought.

"You okay?" he asked.

How could she be okay, when he couldn't spare the time to talk to her on the phone? "Fine," she answered, returning to her view of the fish. Her throat felt rusty from disuse, and she swallowed to clear it. "Who was your meeting with?" Even as she spoke, she berated herself for asking the question. She hadn't intended to ask it. She didn't want him to think she was checking up on him.

"Gus McAvoy and one of his operatives."

Had she imagined the guilt in his voice?

As he entered the room, his reflection appeared on the glass wall of the tank. She watched him drop his shoes, and fling his jacket toward the vanity bench, before he moved to the foot of the bed. The mattress dipped beneath his weight as he sat there, unbuttoning his shirt.

"You like the aquarium, don't you, Jenny? Now that you're used to it."

"I've stopped wearing the earplugs, if that's what you mean."

He yawned and peeled off the shirt. "Was that a yes or a no?"

"A little of both. I like the fish. They're lovely to see, and they have amazingly distinct personalities. But I feel sorry for them, too."

"They seem pretty content to me." Peter stretched out next to her and took a closer look at the aquarium. "They have all the food they can eat, companionship, a controlled environment, and they don't have to worry about predators. What more could a fish want?"

"Privacy."

He glanced at her, smiling quizzically. She tried to smile back and couldn't quite manage it. She lay with her nose only millimeters from the glass, following the flash of the neon tetras.

"I can't wait to get out of this cast." She hadn't meant to say that either, but the admission was wrung from her before she could stop her tongue.

"That reminds me, I have a surprise." Peter hoisted himself off the bed, recovered his jacket and withdrew some folded papers from the inside pocket, which he presented to her with a flourish.

She rolled to her side, propping herself on one elbow while she smoothed out the creases in the papers. They appeared to be some kind of contract. "What's this?"

"An agreement for a rental car."

She stared at him, wide-eyed. "For me?"

"Who else would I be renting a car for?" He lay beside her, close enough that they rubbed shoulders. His hand settled warmly on the curve of her hip. "To save you the eyestrain of reading the fine print, the agreement runs from next Wednesday to the end of March. I figured that would give you time to decide whether you like the car. If you don't, we'll return it. If you do, we have the option to buy."

"What kind of car is it?"

"A Toyota Camry."

"What color?"

"Red. This year's model. Automatic transmission, so you'll be able to drive it once you've got your walking cast. I took it for a test spin and I think you'll like the way it handles. The driver's seat's a little cramped for me, but it should be right for you."

She looked from Peter to the contract, striving to take it all in. She saw the date on the contract. *Today's date.* And comprehension dawned. When Peter phoned that afternoon, he had taken Dee into his confidence.

They were talking about the car, Jenny realized. *That's why Dee was whispering. That's why she was giggling. And I was jealous . . .*

"Oh, Peter!" she cried, and throwing her arms about his neck, she burst into tears.

"Jenny? Honey? What's wrong?"

"N-nothing." He was so sweet and attentive, and she was such an idiot that when he'd come in tonight she'd been too busy wallowing in self-pity to say hello.

He patted her on the back, trying to comfort her. "Listen, honey, I know I should've talked it over with you, but as I said before, if you don't like the car, we'll return it."

"No! I want this one."

"If you want a different color—"

"Red's perfect. I love it. It's absolutely perfect." Surely a man wouldn't choose a red car for a woman he didn't find exciting.

Peter cradled her in his arms and swayed from side to side, rocking her, as the storm of weeping intensified. "If it's perfect, why the tears?"

Because she was relieved. Because she felt guilty. Because she had failed him. But she wouldn't fail him again. Peter deserved her undivided loyalty, and from now she would give him nothing less.

She clung to him, and he gave a shaky laugh. "You're drowning me," he teased.

She buried her face in the curve of his shoulder. "It's because I'm so happy," she said.

FROM THAT NIGHT ON, Jenny counted the hours till her appointment.

On Saturday morning, Raette brought by the books for her to autograph. She said, "You're lookin' better."

"I'm feeling better," Jenny replied. "I have an appointment with the orthopedist on Wednesday, so the next time you see me I'll be in a walking cast."

"That must be a pretty big deal," said Raette. "You ought to have a comin' out party."

"I second the motion," Peter said. "We could make it an open house, have it on Superbowl Sunday."

Jenny laughed and said, "Let's do it."

Peter was out jogging the following morning when Beverly Rudolph came to the door, collecting for one of her causes. While Jenny made out a check, Bev remarked, "I don't know what you said to Rita the other day, but she's been harder than usual to get along with."

"There seems to be a lot of that going around," said Jenny.

"That's the truth. It's practically endemic in this building."

Jenny eyed Bev curiously as she handed over her donation. "If you and Rita don't get along, why do you share an apartment?"

"I can't speak for Rita," Bev replied as she wrote Jenny a receipt. "As for me . . . Well, I guess I'm just a natural born reformer."

Or a glutton for punishment, Jenny thought.

Later that day Toni Greer came by to invite Jenny to a séance. "If we combine forces," Toni said, "I may be able to see more clearly the source of the danger you're in."

"I'll think about it," Jenny replied, although she had no intention of going. Toni had cried wolf too often; her entreaty fell upon deaf ears.

JENNY'S ORTHOPEDIST had two partners, an office near Sutter Memorial Hospital, a waiting room full of patients, and a name that looked like an eye chart.

Peter had planned to hang around while Jenny saw the doctor. After her appointment, he would drive her by the Toyota dealer's to pick up the rented Camry, and from there he would go on about his business. But when Jenny checked in the receptionist informed her, "I'm afraid there'll be a wait. Doctor was called away on an emergency, so we're running a teensy bit behind."

"Which doctor?" Jenny asked in a subtle attempt to find out how his name was pronounced.

"Your doctor," said the receptionist.

So much for subtlety.

"How long a wait are we talking about?" Jenny asked.

"More than an hour, less than a day."

"Does that mean the doctor's not back yet?"

"You got it," said the receptionist. "I don't suppose you'd care to reschedule?"

Jenny gave the woman her X-rays, a copy of Dr. Clancy's notes and an unqualified "no." In return, she was given a questionnaire to fill out.

She reported the gist of this exchange to Peter and added, "It looks as if I'm going to be stuck here awhile. Why don't you go on to the office? I'll give you a call when I'm through."

"No problem," he said. "I brought a briefcase full of work."

But he hadn't brought a chair, and there was standing room only in the reception area.

So much for making plans.

He rounded up a folding chair for Jenny from the office next door, left her in an out-of-the-way corner filling out the questionnaire and went on to his office.

Her appointment was for one-fifteen. She wasn't taken to an examining room till three-forty-five, and as she told Peter later, when they were on their way home, "There was nothing to read but old issues of *Sports Illustrated* and the other patients' casts."

In the examining room she had only a wall chart of the human skeleton and her own cast to read, and that started her thinking.

"I wanted to preserve your proposal," she told Peter. "Keep it as a memento. So when the nurse came in to cut off my cast, I asked if I could make some copies on the copy machine."

The nurse was happy to oblige. "I'll make the copies for you," she said, and went off with the appropriate section of plaster, leaving Jenny alone with the wall chart and her leg, which, once it was unencumbered, she told Peter, "... felt lighter than air."

"How does it look?" Peter asked.

Thin. Pale. Gross. Hairy. The bruising on her ankle had lost its technicolor splendor and was now a putrid yellow. "You don't want to know. Be glad you weren't there. I am."

Peter laughed. He thought she was exaggerating, but she wasn't. She was pleased he hadn't been there to see her leg, even though his company would have helped pass the time.

With no one to talk to and no other diversions, she studied the wall chart. She memorized the names of the bones. "All two hundred and six." She memorized the names of the bony processes and the various types of joints.

During the drive home, when Peter stopped at a red light, she wiggled her fingers in front of his face. "Have you any idea how intricate the hand is?"

Peter grinned and said he hadn't given it much thought. "What happened next?"

"After about forty-five minutes, the radiology tech took me down the hall for X-rays."

She'd accompanied the tech thinking the end was in sight, but she had only begun to wait. Fifteen minutes for the films to be processed. Another twenty because the poor quality of one of the views required a return trip down the hall.

Once the X-rays met with the tech's approval, she was taken to the casting room and abandoned, along with her films.

"When I say 'casting' and 'films' in the same sentence, what's the first thing you think of?" she asked Peter.

"Hollywood," he replied, as they sped along the American River Parkway. "The movie industry."

"Same here," said Jenny. "Or I used to."

But not any more. Not after spending the better part of an hour in the casting room at her orthopedist's office, surrounded by prosthetic appliances, some of which resembled medieval torture devices. Instead of the smell of greasepaint, the odor of plaster dust filled the air. Strips of cloth festooned the walls. The room had no connection to Hollywood, yet it reminded her of Boris Karloff.

"It looked like a place where you'd make mummies," she told Peter. "Not that I'm knocking it, you understand. It's just that I got tired of waiting."

It was twenty minutes to six when the doctor waltzed in, the tails of his lab coat flapping in the breeze. He'd clamped her X-rays, old and new, onto the viewing boxes, scowled at them, grunted his approval, scowled at her leg, manipulated her ankle, grunted something about a tendon being shortened and begun slapping on another cast.

"Not much of a bedside manner," said Peter. "I'm surprised he has so many patients."

"I'm surprised his patients have patience," said Jenny.

The doctor had obviously had a miserable day, so she'd tried not to make matters worse. Taking a page from her mother's book, she had tried to soften him up with flattery. Smiling her winningest smile, she'd inquired, "Has anyone ever told you you look like Boris Karloff?"

"You didn't!" said Peter.

"Yes, I did. Do you think I'd make it up?"

"No, but—"

"Boris Karloff was quite a handsome man, Peter. He was distinguished, soft-spoken, a *gentleman*. I meant it as a compliment."

Peter signaled for a right, downshifted and swung into the horseshoe drive of her apartment complex. "Did your doctor take it that way?"

Jenny sighed and admitted he hadn't. Not that it made much difference. A scowl was a scowl. A grunt was a grunt. And he could hardly kick her out. That would have been unprofessional. So he'd finished applying the cast, and when he was through she'd said, "Thank you Doctor," and let it go at that because in all that trying day no one had given her a clue how to pronounce his name.

By then it was after six. Peter was waiting for her in the outer office, but the Toyota dealer was closed. She wouldn't be able to pick up the Camry till tomorrow. But that was a minor delay. What did it matter? She had her walking cast.

As Peter helped her out of the car she said, "Now all I have to do is learn how to use it."

The new cast had a metal foot plate, which made it feel heavier than the old one. And of course it would take a while for the plaster to dry. Then, too, she was still somewhat leery about putting her weight on her left leg, but time and experience would remedy that.

In the meantime, she had the crutches to give her confidence. She felt secure using them, even on the stairs.

When Peter offered assistance, she waved him off. "I need the practice," she said.

When she stopped for a breather, midway to the second floor, she urged him to go on ahead. Her energy had flagged, but not her spirits. "Give me a week and I'll race you."

Once she got her second wind, her optimism was enough to carry her to the top of the stairs, but as she started along the corridor, she saw Peter striding toward her.

"What's going on?" she inquired, laughing. And then she saw the other tenants milling about outside her door, and Peter's grim expression, and the laughter died in her throat. "Something's wrong. What is it?"

Peter moved to the center of the hallway, blocking her path. "C'mon. I'll take you to dinner."

"Dinner? But we just got here." She tried to get past him, but he made a cage of his arms and shepherded her toward the stairs.

"Please, honey, let's get out of here."

She shook her head fiercely, resisting. "I'm not going anywhere till you tell me what's happened."

"It's your apartment," he said with a harshness that gave his reply the impact of a body blow. "Someone's trashed your apartment."

Chapter Twelve

Lurine Watley, one of the flight attendants from across the hall, had discovered the crime. "I was on my way out and I noticed your door was ajar," she told Jenny. "So I knocked, and when no one answered I looked in. As soon as I saw what had happened, I called Toni Greer."

Toni had informed the police less than half an hour before Peter and Jenny got home. Peter used Lurine's phone to call Gus McAvoy, the private investigator who worked for his law firm, who arrived within minutes of the officers. He went directly to the apartment, and a short time later returned to take Jenny's fingerprints.

"A formality," he explained. "I took Peter's, too. I'm dusting for prints, and this'll help weed out any that don't legitimately belong in your apartment."

Several of the neighbors, Lurine among them, offered Jenny the hospitality of their own living rooms. She declined each invitation with an adamant shake of her head and sat quietly at the top of the stairs, waiting to be summoned, dreading what she might find when she was summoned.

On the surface she appeared calm, but that was only on the surface. Inside she was shivering.

She was shivering on the outside, too, by the time Peter came to fetch her.

He helped her to her feet, draped his jacket around her shoulders and ushered her along the corridor, describing the scene she was about to see. But his description didn't prepare her for the destruction of her apartment.

She stood in the entryway, a reluctant witness, stunned by the sea of papers that covered the floor. "My files!"

"Yes, ma'am," said the older detective. "That's what Mr. Darien was telling us, but it looks to me like most of them can be salvaged."

His partner muttered agreement, and Gus McAvoy said, "That's right."

Jenny looked to Peter for confirmation, and he nodded. With a consoling hand on her shoulder, he guided her through the chaos.

Pictures hung askew, occasional tables were overturned and lamps upended. Stuffing spilled from slashes in the love seat, in the chair and sofa cushions. Books and videocassettes and record albums had been dumped off their shelves and strewn about willy-nilly, and her own books—the biographies she had written—lay face down, spines broken, pages trampled.

Soot from the fireplace smeared the walls, and in the dining room the set of fireplace tools had been planted carefully as a trophy atop shards of china and broken crystal.

Jenny sagged against the armrests of the crutches and reached for Peter's hand. Her fingers felt icy against the warmth of his palm. "The kitchen?"

"More of the same." His voice was gentle, as if to ease the shock.

"The office?"

"It's ... pretty bad."

She glanced around the living room. "Worse than this?"

"They, uh ... Whoever did this got your computer."

"Wha—what about the disks?"

"I'm sorry, honey. Those, too."

"Ma'am?" said the older detective. "There's something in the bedroom I think you should take a look at."

The aquarium! She closed her eyes for a moment, and sent up a silent prayer. *Please, God! Not Emmett. Not the angelfish. Not the tetras.*

Expecting the worst, she set off across the living room. Her legs threatened to give way with every step. If only she could stop shivering! When she reached the hallway, she lost her footing and would have fallen if Peter hadn't steadied her.

"Easy, honey," he whispered, sensing her apprehension. "The fish are okay. Fat and sassy as ever."

She tried to smile, but her mouth wouldn't cooperate until she entered the bedroom and saw for herself that the aquarium had not been touched. "Oh, Peter, I thought ... I was so afraid ... But they don't even look hungry!"

"Ma'am, this is what I wanted to show you."

She turned toward the detective, registering the open closet doors, the hangers, now empty, that had once held her wardrobe, the piles of soiled, shredded rags scattered upon the carpet ...

They looked like ... No, they couldn't be ... But they were her clothes!

And then she saw the message that was scrawled in lurid red upon the wall:

HATE—TO LOATH AND DESPISE WITH
GREAT MALISE.
SYN. JENIFER SPALDING

Her stomach gave a sickening lurch. Her heart leaped
into her throat. "Is that— Is it—"

"It's spray paint," said Gus McAvoy. "But I'll give
you dollars to doughnuts, whoever wrote it wanted it to
be mistaken for blood."

"By me," said Jenny.

"Yes, ma'am," said the detective. "It looks as if
you're the target of this break-in—although strictly
speaking, we haven't found any signs of a break-in.
Nothing appears to have been stolen—leastways nothing obvious. A burglar would've taken the computer,
instead of smashing it. Same goes for the TV and VCR
and... Well, you get the picture. Whoever ransacked
this place went straight for your stuff and left Mr. Darien's things alone. So I've gotta ask, do you know of
anyone who might have a grudge against you?"

"No, I don't."

His partner assumed the role of "bad cop" with a
tight-lipped smile. "No ex-husbands? No old boy-
friends? No jealous lovers you're seeing on the side?"

"No! No one like that."

The smile became a smirk. "You sure about that?"
he demanded. "If you're having an extracurricular affair, you might as well tell us and save everyone concerned a major hassle."

"Make it easy on yourself, Ms. Spaulding." This advice came from the good cop. "If you want to talk privately, all you have to do is say so. Detective Greeley
here will take Mr. Darien into the next room, and see
that we're not interrupted."

Peter's arms went around her, forming a shield. "She's answered your question. We both have."

The good cop scratched the back of his neck. "Let's get back to this message, ma'am. Do you notice anything unusual about it?"

"Unusual?" Jenny cried, on a note of rising agitation. "It's in my *bedroom*. On my *wall*. It's addressed to *me*. *Everything* about it is unusual."

"Jenny," said Peter. "I think what Detective Yeager is referring to is the fact that your name is misspelled."

"It's not just my name, Peter. Every other *word* is misspelled!"

"But isn't that the way your name was written on that fan letter?"

"Yes, it is." He'd seen the envelope. How could she deny it?

"What was in the letter, honey? Who was it from?"

Her eyes shied away from Peter's. She hesitated, at a loss, not wanting to hurt him, and knowing she must. Telling him about the letter under these conditions would be like giving him a slap in the face. Yet she had to tell him. The police had to know. And she'd have to produce the letter—if it still existed—to allay their suspicions. To convince them that neither she nor Peter had anything to do with this . . . this *devastation*. To prove that her anonymous correspondent was the most likely suspect.

The *only* suspect.

Her gaze flew to the message, then sought Gus McAvoy's. He responded by reaching into his coat pocket for a leather-bound notebook, which he flipped open, displaying an envelope—

He'd found the note! Not only found it, but kept it to himself, she realized as he mimed locking his lips with a key.

Whether she kept her secret or told it, Gus McAvoy would abide by her wishes.

His conspiratorial wink restored her confidence and gave her the strength to turn her back on the detectives and look at Peter. To focus on him to the exclusion of all others. To talk to him as if the two of them were alone. To have faith that Peter would understand and trust that he would forgive.

WHILE SHE WAS AT IT, Jenny made a clean breast of things by including the story of Toni Greer's predictions. Her explanation was exhaustive enough to cover all the bases, thorough enough to anticipate any questions, but inevitably there were questions she didn't foresee.

One was her own, and concerned Peter's reaction. She had expected him to be surprised, upset, perhaps even furious. She had expected bruised pride, heated objections and a few recriminations. What she got was a lukewarm facsimile.

"How can we have anything between us if we're not honest with each other?" Peter said.

"I have a right to know the bad as well as the good," he said.

"I don't need your protection," he said. "From now on, don't try to spare my feelings."

When all was said and done, however, Peter's verbal slaps on the wrist were far less passionate than Jenny would have desired.

And less spontaneous?

Perhaps.

The words might ring true, but the emotions seemed false, and she was left with the feeling that his protests had been rehearsed, as if he'd known about the letter all along.

But the only way he could have known was through Dee. Had she taken the letter deliberately? Had she shown it to Peter, hoping to drive a wedge between them?

The obvious answer was "Yes," but Jenny didn't accept it. She *couldn't* accept it.

Detective Yeager had questions, one of which arose from the absence of postage on the anonymous note. "After what's happened today, let's assume the note was slipped in with the fan mail while the package was in the vestibule."

Sitting in the ruins of her apartment, Jenny said she couldn't quibble with that.

"So who has access to the vestibule?" he asked.

Tenants and their guests, she told him. And since the locks weren't changed when apartments changed hands, former tenants. Then there were the owners and the management staff and the maintenance crew, past and present. There were delivery people and tradespeople, plumbers and electricians, men who installed telephones and cable TV, and those who tended aquariums. There were cleaning people, salesmen, solicitors and political activists. As an afterthought, she added the information that a number of the current residents let in anyone who buzzed, without bothering to ask for their credentials.

"Now that I think about it," she said, "practically anyone can get into this building."

"What about your apartment?" Yeager asked. "Who has access to it?"

"Wait a minute," said Greeley before Jenny could reply. "I thought we'd established that entry was gained from the balcony."

"And I thought we'd established that the door to the balcony was locked." Peter spoke as if he were weary of repeating this argument. "I double-checked it myself before we left this afternoon and the floor bolt was fastened. The door couldn't have been opened more than an inch or two."

Greeley scowled and shook his head. "I'm telling you, Mr. Darien, that door was wide open when we got here."

"And I'm telling you, somebody else must've opened it," Peter insisted.

"Dee," said Jenny, and for the benefit of the detectives spelled Dee's full name, and added, "She's my research assistant."

"Dee wasn't here," Peter said. "You told me you'd sent her to the library."

"She might have come back," Jenny said.

"Does she have a key?" Detective Yeager asked.

Jenny had to admit Dee didn't.

"Who does?" Yeager asked.

"Peter and I, of course, and Toni Greer. She's the manager-slash-leasing agent."

"And that's it?"

"That's all we're aware of," said Peter. "But Jenny keeps a spare key hanging on a Peg-Board in the pantry. If anybody wanted to get in, it would be a snap to borrow the spare and have a copy made, and no one would be the wiser."

"One last question, Ms. Spaulding," Yeager said. "Who knew you were going to be gone this afternoon?"

"I was so happy about the walking cast, I told almost everyone I know I'd be seeing the doctor today," Jenny answered. When Yeager looked up from his notepad, she added a crestfallen, "I'm sorry, Detective. I haven't been much help."

"Don't be so hard on yourself," Gus McAvoy said. "There's more than one way to narrow down a list of suspects." His voice boomed with confidence as he went on. "To begin with, I'd like to point out that whoever vandalized this place sure as hell went about it methodically. The perpetrator seems to have known which belongings are yours and which are Pete's, right down to the aquarium, which I understand is a recent acquisition."

"I see what you're driving at," Peter said. "Whoever did this must be familiar with the apartment."

"And even more familiar with Jenny," McAvoy continued. "He knew where he could inflict the most damage. He went for her files, her disks, her computer, her books—"

"That's kind of a paradox," Peter broke in.

"How do you mean?" Jenny inquired.

"Look at the note, honey. What strikes you about it?"

She studied the note, frowned, shook her head. "I give up."

"Look at the way it's composed. It reads as if it's copied from a dictionary. So why the cut-and-paste job? Why not just take a paperback dictionary and cut out the whole definition?"

"'Cause he loves books," said McAvoy. "He treats 'em with respect."

"Not mine," said Jenny.

Detective Greeley's questions were personal. Some of them bordered on being offensive. How long had she known Peter? How long had they been "close?" Had she ever stepped out on him? Had she ever *thought* about stepping out on him?

No? Well, didn't she sometimes *look* at other men? Didn't she occasionally find one of those other men attractive, maybe even speculate about him, fantasize about him? If not, what was wrong with her? If so, what was it about a man that turned her on?

Jenny responded to this inquisition as candidly as she could, even though she couldn't see that it would lead anywhere. She didn't figure out why Greeley should be so interested in her love life until he and his partner were preparing to leave, and Greeley took her aside, gave her his card, and asked her to give him a call if it turned out that anything had been stolen.

"Give me a call either way," he said. "Maybe we could get together for coffee or a matinee."

Jenny was amazed by this turn of events, but Gus McAvoy wasn't. "I knew Greeley was gonna hit on you."

"How?" she asked. "How could you tell?"

McAvoy tapped a forefinger to the corner of his eye. "I'm a private investigator—a trained observer. It's my business to know these things."

Before Jenny could pursue the subject, Gus announced he'd missed supper and was hungry enough to eat a bear. "I'm gonna go out and get us a pizza. How do you like it?"

"Without anchovies," Jenny said.

Peter grinned and said, "Same here, and while you're at it, would you pick up some beer?"

When McAvoy left, by tacit agreement, they set about restoring a semblance of order to the living room. Peter wrestled the coffee table and chairs into place and put the cushions back on the love seat and sofa. Jenny busied herself with the sea of papers.

They had worked steadily for several minutes before she paused to contemplate the immensity of the task that lay ahead. Sighing, she bent down to pick up a manila folder, and as she straightened, she glanced at Peter. He was still grinning.

"I suppose you're going to claim you knew it, too," she said.

"If you're referring to Greeley's proposition, the answer's yes. I saw it coming all evening."

"Why didn't you say something? Doesn't it bother you that he asked me out?"

"Not as long as you turned him down." Peter set a lamp on its end table and straightened the shade, studying her all the while. "Your trouble, Jenny, is your self-image is out of kilter. Don't you know what a knockout you are?"

She wrinkled her nose at him. "Why don't you refresh my memory?"

Peter's grin widened. His eyes danced with amusement. "Do you remember that morning at the ski lodge, when I waited for you in the lobby?"

"Vaguely."

"Well, I watched you come down the stairs, and I saw the way every guy you passed turned to look at you. I knew they were wondering if you were available, thinking 'Wow! What a great looking lady.'"

"I think it's starting to come back to me now."

"There were all these men admiring you, and you didn't even notice. It gave me such a kick, I wanted to crow, 'Tough luck, fellas, you can't have her. She's with me.'"

"More, more!"

Peter laughed and sat on the edge of the coffee table. He caught hold of Jenny's wrist, and with an easy tug hauled her onto his lap. "You're not only gorgeous. You're modest, as well. It's no wonder I'm crazy about you."

She hugged him, sighing with pleasure. "The feeling's mutual, my darling."

"Is it?"

"You better believe it."

"Convince me."

She smiled and dug the copy of his proposal out of her pocket. "If you want proof, here it is." She handed him the paper. "Would I have kept that if I didn't love you?"

He unfolded the copy, glanced at it, and gave it back to her. "I'm afraid it's going to take more than that."

"You must be joking," she said. But when she looked at him, she saw that he was serious. She held out one hand in a gesture of supplication, pleading with him to believe her. "If you don't know you're everything to me, how can I convince you?"

"It's relatively simple, honey. All you have to do is go public with our engagement."

She stared at him, her eyes tragic. "Y-you mean tell Phyllis?"

"You've gotta start someplace." He framed her face between his palms. "Listen, Jenny, I want you to be my wife. I have no doubts about that. No qualms. No reservations. And I don't want to keep it a secret. I want to tell my mother, my uncle, Gus, the people I work with. I want the world to know we're getting married. But if you're not sure—''

"I'm sure, Peter. Really, I am. I've never been more certain of anything in my life. You want to tell the world and so do I—''

"But you don't want to tell your mother.''

Jenny shook her head. "It's not that I don't *want* to tell her. It's just that Phyllis isn't exactly in favor of marriage. At least, not for women." *And especially not for her daughter.* "I don't know how she'll take it when she finds out we're engaged.''

Which glanced off the truth without hitting it head-on, thank heaven. What would Peter say, if she told him that Phyllis was livid on the subject of marriage? For as long as Jenny could remember, her mother had never used the word without adding the suffix *trap.*

Peter's hands moved to her shoulders. "If you're worried that she won't approve, I think you're borrowing trouble. Phyllis seems to like me, honey.''

Phyllis also seemed to believe that every waiter she chanced to encounter was the spitting image of Cary Grant or Kevin Costner or whichever celebrity would fill the bill. But that was her inimitable way of guaranteeing superior service; a game she played for public consumption. Privately, she believed men were shallow, egotistical creatures, who were much too easily swayed by a kind remark or a pretty face.

But however Phyllis took the news—whatever ruckus she raised—sooner or later she had to be told that her daughter was getting married. *And it's up to me to do the honors,* Jenny thought.

"Cheer up, honey." Peter brushed his knuckles along the point of her chin. "Could be Phyllis has mellowed. Maybe she'll surprise you.''

"Maybe she will," Jenny allowed, although to her it didn't seem likely. But whether Phyllis had mellowed or not, the time had come to bite the bullet. "I'll call her tomorrow and tell her."

IT WAS TEN-FIFTEEN and the three of them were haggling over the last slice of pizza when Toni Greer dropped in to assess the damages to the apartment. When she saw the living room, she looked more morose than usual.

"This is dreadful," she declared. "Simply dreadful. We've never had a break-in before. I hope you won't hold us responsible."

"It's too early to address the issue of responsibility," Peter answered in legalese. "We'll have to wait till we have more information. It's possible the police will turn up evidence of negligence on the part of the management company."

While Toni was still reeling from the implications of his reply, he said, "It goes without saying we'll want the locks changed as quickly as possible, and I expect you'll expedite arrangements to have the place repainted."

"Yes, of course," she agreed. "That's the main reason I'm here. To see what repairs you'll need."

"And the other reason?"

"That has to do with a séance I'm planning. In light of what's happened, I thought perhaps Jennifer might have decided to attend."

Jenny hadn't, and if she'd had the opportunity she would have said so, but before she could speak out Peter asked Toni, "What's the point of going to a séance now? Wouldn't it be akin to locking the barn door after the horse is stolen?"

"No, Mr. Darien. Quite the contrary. The horse, as you so colorfully put it, is still in his stall, but I can't say how long he will remain there. He—or to be accurate, I should say *she*—is in the gravest imaginable danger."

"I see," said Peter. "When is this séance?"

"This Friday evening at nine o'clock, and I do mean nine sharp. I'm something of a stickler for punctuality."

"And where is it?"

"My apartment. Needless to say, you're welcome to come along, if you like."

"In that case," said Peter, "we'll be there."

Chapter Thirteen

It was well past midnight before McAvoy departed. The instant the door closed behind him, Jenny said, "Tell me why, Peter. Why should we go to this séance? Give me one good reason."

"I can think of several, honey, all of them winners." Peter proceeded to tick them off on his fingers. "First, we might learn something useful. Second, as long as you're under threat, we're in no position to pass up any chance, however slim, of uncovering information. Third, the Widow Greer has a key to this place, which means it's possible she's the culprit, or fourth, she knows who the culprit is."

There was an eloquent silence while these arguments sank in. Finally, resigned to the inevitable, Jenny finished, "And then there's a fifth. All of the above."

Peter eyed her skeptically. "Is it settled, then? No more protests?"

"No more protests. I'll go to the séance with you, but right now I'm going to have a bath." She headed for the bedroom and he fell into step beside her.

"Scrub your back, lady?"

She gave him a flirtatious, sidelong glance and replied in a throaty whisper. "Best offer I've had all day."

PETER STAYED HOME FROM the office the following morning to deal with the insurance adjuster, the locksmith and the Toyota dealer. He and Jenny had agreed to pick up the car that evening.

Dee reported for work at her regular time and seemed genuinely shocked by the state of the apartment. She wandered from room to room, wringing her hands, shaking her head, so distraught she could barely speak.

Her performance was convincing, but it didn't allay Jenny's suspicions. Not entirely. And when Dee set to work on the files, Jenny remained undecided whether Dee was a consummate actress or if she'd had nothing to do with the break-in.

Bev Rudolph was next to appear. She stopped by to inquire how they were doing, and stayed to clean up the kitchen.

At mid-morning, Jenny was sifting through the wreckage of her wardrobe, searching for any garments that might be salvaged and mourning the loss of others, when Lila Darien came into the bedroom and wrapped her in motherly arms.

"Did Peter tell you—"

"Yes, he did, Jennifer, and I'm positively ecstatic! I've always wanted a daughter, and now I'm actually going to have one. And I have such wonderful ideas for the wedding. Wait'll you hear—"

Lila stopped suddenly, and held Jenny at arms' length. In the blink of an eye, she went from joy to sadness. "But my dear, this... *disaster* that happened last night. What a horrible experience it must've been, to come home and find all this." She made a sweeping gesture around the room with one hand. "I am so very sorry."

Her concern was very nearly Jenny's undoing. Tears stung the backs of her eyes and she blinked them away, but she couldn't keep the quaver from her voice, as she said, "The worst of it is, there's so much to do, I don't know where to begin."

Lila surveyed the vacant closet, the empty bureau drawers, the heaps of tattered clothing on the floor. She took in the way Jenny was dressed—faded jeans, out at the knees and split along one side seam to fit over her cast, Peter's old Stanford T-shirt, the walking cast on one foot, a rubber-soled thong on the other.

"Obviously, you're going to need a few things to wear."

"Obviously," Jenny echoed.

"From the skin out?"

"Aside from a few things in the bathroom hamper, everything's gone." Jenny held up a lacy scrap of material. "Whoever did this got my undies...even got my *shoes!*"

"What a shame," Lila sympathized, and then, more briskly, "but you know, Jennifer, there are loads of women who would envy your predicament. Think how much fun it'll be picking out your trousseau. In the meantime, if you'll make a list of your sizes, I'll go out and get enough things to keep you going. And while you're making your list, I'll see what's needed in the kitchen. As long as I'm going shopping, I may as well do it right."

It was noon before the insurance man completed his inventory. Soon afterward, Peter left for the office; fifteen minutes later, Lila collected Jenny's list and announced she was leaving for the mall. Beverly and Dee joined the exodus, and by twelve-thirty, Jenny had the apartment to herself.

She went to the phone, then hesitated, filled with uncertainty. With the time difference, in New Haven it would be three-thirty. Should she try to reach her mother at work, or wait till this evening and call her at home?

At work, Jenny decided. Phyllis would be less apt to make a fuss with her fellow Realtors looking on.

She picked up the receiver and dialed the number before she could change her mind, and while she waited for the call to go through, she recalled Lila saying, *"If you want a reconciliation, where you begin doesn't matter. What's important is that you make the attempt..."*

But Jenny knew from experience where she began with her mother *did* matter. It could make all the difference, and so she had psyched herself up for this moment through a long, sleepless night. She knew precisely what she wanted to say and how she should say it.

She had prepared a speech carefully, until she could recite it word for word, but when Phyllis came on the line, Jenny was overcome by emotion. Her mind went blank. When she opened her mouth, all she could manage was a plaintive, "Mom? Is that you? Golly, it's good to hear your voice."

"Perhaps you should call me more often."

"I know I should." Even as she spoke, Jenny was astounded that, for the first time since she'd become an adolescent, she had conceded a point to her mother.

"Yes. Well, I suppose I shouldn't complain. Some of my friends never hear from their children. Or if they do, it's because the kids need money."

Phyllis must be astonished, too. She usually played the long-suffering mother to the hilt. It wasn't like her to back off, much less make excuses for her neglectful daughter.

"I, uh—Mom?" Jenny began, and then she could go no further.

"Yes, dear, what is it? You don't need money, do you?"

"No, but I need your blessing."

"My *blessing?* Oh, my God! You and Peter—"

"We're engaged, Mom. We're getting married."

"Well, well, *well,*" said Phyllis, a hint of frost in her tone. "When did all this happen?"

"Within the last couple of weeks."

"That long? And you waited till now to tell me?"

The frost had become glacial, but Jenny told herself, *You knew this wouldn't be easy.* "We didn't tell anyone till today. You're the first to know."

"What about Peter's mother? Doesn't she know?"

"Yes, but you're the first one I've told."

Phyllis responded with a martyred sigh.

It's never too late to try, Jenny thought. *Whatever else happens, don't lose your temper.* "We set the wedding date last night. March twenty-first."

"That's my birthday!"

"Yes, Mom. That's why we chose it."

"So I take it I'm invited."

"Of course you are. You're my mother. You're the only family I have, and Peter's eager to meet you. You can't seriously think we wouldn't ask you to our wedding."

"Frankly, dear, after the way I've carried on about marriage—"

"Mom, before you go on, there's something I have to say to you. Something I should have told you years ago. I've been doing a lot of thinking lately. About you and

Daddy and me. And I've thought about what it must've been like for you, having so much potential, your whole life ahead of you, being the prettiest girl in your high-school class and valedictorian to boot, the girl who won every award in sight, the one who was voted most likely to succeed. And then two months after graduation, you met Daddy, and a few months after that you found out you were pregnant, and by the following year you were married and had me, and you weren't even nineteen."

"Who put you up to this?" Phyllis demanded. "This call was Peter's idea, wasn't it?"

"Peter insisted that I call you, but he didn't tell me what to say." Before her mother could raise further arguments, Jenny rushed on. "I've tried to imagine how you must have felt, watching other girls, not as bright, not as pretty, go to dances and parties, go off to college—do all the things you'd dreamed of doing, and know you couldn't do them yourself because you had a baby to take care of. And after Daddy left, when you were working days and taking real-estate courses nights, you managed to keep your act together. And with all those responsibilities, somehow...*somehow*...you never blamed *me*."

Another sigh from Phyllis, not at all martyred. Almost like a releasing of tension. "None of it was your fault, Jenny. I had to make a choice, not just for your sake, but for mine. I couldn't go on living from hand to mouth, from payday to payday, especially when there were so many times when it was a long while between paydays. Your father would be flush one week, broke the next, and I could never get him to plan ahead. He didn't mind the insecurity, didn't even notice it, and I resented that. I resented him for not seeing how desperate I was, for putting me in a position where I had to make the choice.''

''But you didn't resent me, Mom. You *loved* me, and you had ambitions for me. You wanted me to have advantages you'd never had. The kind of home, the kind of stability, the education, the career...all the opportunities you'd missed out on. I never appreciated how difficult it must've been for you till I met Peter. And the past two weeks, since we've talked about getting married, I've been thinking about having children, and—Well, to be honest, the idea's kind of scary.''

''Doesn't Peter want children?''

''Yes, and so do I. I mean, I want to have a baby. That part's fine. But once the baby's born, you have to change your priorities because you're responsible for this little person. You're not free to go places on the spur of the moment or do things on a whim. And being in a cast has given me a taste of what that's like, except that a cast doesn't require constant attention. You don't have to feed it at two in the morning. You don't have to burp it and bathe it and change its diapers and walk the floor with it when it has a tummy ache—''

''A cast doesn't snuggle up to you, either. It doesn't have hair soft as thistledown and big, trusting eyes. A cast doesn't have a gummy smile that melts your heart. It doesn't give you big wet kisses. It doesn't wriggle all over the moment you walk into a room and hold its arms out to you to be picked up.'' Phyllis sighed again, and this time she sounded nostalgic. ''I may not have been any great shakes as a mother, Jenny, but I promise you I'll be one heck of a grandma.''

''But you were!'' Jenny cried. ''You were a good mother. That's what I wanted to tell you. I only hope I can be half as unselfish, half as patient and forgiving as you've been. I want to be the best mother I can be and the best possible wife, only I'm not sure I've got what it takes, and I'm ten years older than you were when I was born.''

"My youth worked in my favor, dear. I didn't have time to worry about what I was getting into or what kind of mother I'd be. If I'd thought about it, I'd have been terrified, but you came along before I was grown up enough to realize I ought to be worried. And once you were born, I sort of learned as I went. But I think that's something all new mothers go through.''

After a reflective silence, Phyllis went on. ''I remember someone gave me a copy of *Baby and Child Care,* and I read that book till I wore it out. Dr. Spock said raising kids was mostly common sense, and that I knew more about babies than I thought I did. He also made a point of saying how resilient babies are, which turned out to be true, thank goodness, because being a parent seemed awfully trial-and-error to me, yet look how well you've turned out.''

"And that makes it worth all the sacrifice?''

"Who said anything about sacrifice?'' Phyllis hooted with laughter. ''Don't get me wrong. I'm not saying it was a cakewalk, being a mother. Just following a toddler around all day requires a huge investment of time and energy. But I'll have you know, Jennifer Spaulding, soon to be Darien, I have never regretted investing in you. There's nothing more fulfilling than seeing your daughter grow up to be a fine young woman. And if that doesn't seem like a fair exchange, don't forget I have the East Coast bragging rights to you, my future son-in-law, the lawyer, and to the children you and Peter have.''

"Then you'll have to come to the wedding to protect your interests," said Jenny.

"What kind of wedding are you planning?"

"Peter and I haven't really discussed it yet."

"Don't you think you should? You don't have an abundance of time."

"We'll get round to it, Mom. I'd like a church wedding, with candles and flowers, but I don't think either of us wants anything elaborate. Peter's your typical laid-back Californian, and I'd rather keep the ceremony simple and fairly intimate, so we'll probably limit the guest list to family and our closest friends."

"What about the reception?"

Jenny had to confess she hadn't given any thought to what came after the nuptials. Her fantasies were quite detailed until she stood beside Peter at the altar. There they stopped and never went beyond the "I do's." But as an added inducement, she told her mother, "We're open to suggestions."

"Well, I never…" Phyllis murmured. "This must be a bad connection. I could swear you just asked for my advice."

"I'm asking for more than that. As I said before, I'd like to have your blessing."

"You've always had that, Jennifer."

"Then you'll come out for the wedding?"

"I'll be there," said Phyllis. "A team of wild horses couldn't keep me away."

LILA RETURNED SHORTLY after three o'clock with an array of lingerie and a carload of outerwear for Jenny's approval. "You can keep the outfits you like," she explained. "The ones you don't, I'll take back."

Jenny chose a stitch-pleated skirt and an ivory-and-black tunic-length sweater, a paisley-print dress in pink and taupe, topped with a pink double-breasted waist-length jacket. She chose a divided skirt, a wraparound skirt, some blouses and T-shirts, an unstructured peri-winkle jacket and a jumpsuit and a pair of stirrup pants that she wouldn't be able to wear until she was out of the cast. She chose shoes, belts, scarves—even costume jewelry—marveling at Lila's thoroughness.

"You've thought of everything," she said.

"I had a ball," Lila replied, "and now that we've covered the essentials, wait till you see what I bring you tomorrow."

Peter arrived for the end of the fashion show, and when Lila left he took Jenny to pick up her rental car.

The flowers were delivered that evening, not long after they got back from the Toyota dealer's.

"How beautiful," Jenny exclaimed when she saw the dozen long-stemmed roses. She gathered up the bouquet and cradled the blooms to her face, luxuriating in their delicate perfume and in their lush red color. "First the Camry, and now this! It's too much, Peter. You shouldn't have."

"I didn't," he replied.

She studied the roses, perplexed. "If you didn't send them, who did?"

"Claude, maybe? Max? My mother? Your mother?" Peter shook his head. His expression darkened. "They better not be from Greeley."

She made a face at him, and he grinned. "Look in the box. There must be a card."

Jenny opened the box and found the card, which was hidden in a nest of green paper. She glanced at the message, paled and handed the card to Peter, who read it aloud.

"With sympathy on your recent loss." His voice gruff with outrage, he declared, "They're from the creep who broke in here last night."

While he placed a telephone call to the florist, she crammed the roses back in their carton.

Now that she knew who the flowers were from, it seemed to her they were the color of blood, and they were no longer beautiful. They were hateful! Noxious. She couldn't bear the scent. They symbolized an invasion of her privacy, attempts to terrorize her, to threaten Peter. She wouldn't feel safe until she disposed of every last petal.

Her breath came in ragged gasps as she made her way to the kitchen and dumped the box in the trash compactor. She closed the bin, flipped the wall switch and listened to the mechanical grinding noises the compactor made. When the cycle was finished, she flipped the switch on again. But even knowing that the appliance would destroy the bouquet—would crush the roses beyond recognition—gave her no satisfaction.

Who? her mind shrieked. *Who had done this? Who had stolen into her apartment and violated her things? Who had left the message on the bedroom wall? Who was trying to frighten her? And why? What purpose did it serve?*

By the time she returned to the living room, Peter had completed his call. He put an arm about her and led her to the sofa.

"Who?" she inquired when they were seated. "Who sent the roses?"

"I wish I knew."

"But the florist—"

"Couldn't tell me a thing. He took the order over the phone."

"Then it must have been charged to a credit card!"

Peter nodded, cleared his throat. "It was charged to a Visa card, Jenny. *Your* Visa card."

"That's impossible! I didn't—"

"Shh." Peter drew her close, quieting her outcry. "You don't have to tell me you didn't send those flowers, honey. I know you didn't."

"But they're charged to me!"

"By our intruder, no doubt. When's the last time you used that card?"

"It's been two or three weeks, anyway. Maybe as long as a month."

"Where do you keep it?"

"With my checkbook. The front of the folder has those see-through plastic compartments for credit cards and ID. I transfer the folder to whichever handbag I'm using."

"You haven't been carrying a handbag lately."

"No. Not since I've been on crutches."

"So which bag would your checkbook be in?"

She lifted a hand to her temple, absently rubbed it. "The navy calf shoulder bag, I think. It should be on the shelf in the guest closet."

Peter was already on his feet, heading for the entry hall. Within seconds, he returned with the bag. She opened it, removed the checkbook, found the plastic compartments empty and let out a pent-up breath.

"My Visa card's missing. *Everything* is."

"What else was in there?"

She closed her eyes, remembering. "Several other credit cards, my bank card, insurance, health, library cards, Writers' Guild membership card, a plasticized copy of my birth certificate, and I usually keep my driver's license in the section nearest the checkbook, but I expected to be driving home from the doctor's office yesterday, so I took it with me."

"Any cash?"

She opened her eyes and peered into the zippered section behind the checkbook. "Thirty-two dollars."

"So theft wasn't a motive."

Jenny met Peter's gaze. "What now?"

"We'll have to notify the companies that your credit cards have been stolen."

"I'll call them right away."

"We should also inform the police, and with your permission I'd like to bring Gus in on this. But before we do that I think it would be a good idea to check your files and make sure no other personal papers are missing."

"Yes, of course, Peter. Whatever you say."

As she dropped the checkbook into her handbag, an oblong slip of paper fell out. She picked it up, glanced at it, and recognized the receipt Bev Rudolph had given her for her donation to—

She knitted her brows, trying to decipher the name of the organization, and then she saw the way her name was spelled.

One *n* in Jennifer. No *u* in Spaulding.

Just as it was in the anonymous letter. Just as it was on her bedroom wall.

Chapter Fourteen

They met with Gus McAvoy later that night in the conference room at Peter's office.

McAvoy examined the receipt and the florist's card, and made copies of them for his files. The police, he said, would want the originals. He propped a corkboard on an easel and thumbtacked pieces of evidence to it for display.

A mug of coffee in one hand, he compared his copies of the receipt and the letter with the photograph he'd taken of the lines spray-painted on the bedroom wall.

"What we have here," he said at last, "is handwriting that doesn't match."

"How can you be sure?" Peter demanded. "The receipt's made out in cursive, the notes are block-printed."

"Notice the way the letters slant? The receipt was written by a southpaw. The notes were printed by a subject who's right-handed."

"B-but all three have the same misspelling of my name," Jenny sputtered.

"The spelling's atrocious, I'll grant you that, but in the case of the receipt, it's not a crime."

Peter frowned at the exhibits, making his own comparison. "Is it possible we have a subject who wrote the notes with one hand and the receipt with the other?"

"I wouldn't rule that out, Pete, and I sure as hell wouldn't cross Rudolph off our list of suspects." McAvoy moved to the chalkboard and wrote Beverly Rudolph's name in the topmost corner, then drew vertical lines, dividing the board into thirds. In the far right column, he wrote "Greer's prediction," and beneath that "Brakes fail," and beneath that "Binding breaks," and beneath that "Mail tampered with—letter arrives," and beneath that, "Apartment burgled," and beneath that, "Sympathy note."

"What was missing from your files?" he asked Jenny.

"My college diploma and teaching certificate and my passport. I haven't been able to find my hairbrush, either, or the *Case Studies* book Peter bought for me."

The investigator wrote these on his chart, along with the items taken from her handbag, then stepped away from the chalkboard to consider his outline of events. After a half minute or so, he turned to Jenny. "Have there been any other incidents? Anything that could be construed as a physical threat?"

Jenny considered mentioning Dee's coming to work for her. She thought of the stories Rita had told about the rendezvous between Dee and Peter, but neither of those events could be classified as threatening in the way Gus meant. "No," she answered, "Nothing I can think of."

"Next question," said McAvoy, moving to the center of the board. "What do we know about our perpetrator?"

"She's a recent acquaintance, but not too recent," Jenny replied.

"Why do you say 'not too recent?'"

"She must have been watching me for some time before we actually met. Long enough to gain access to my apartment and become familiar with my routine."

While the investigator was filling in Jenny's speculations, Peter smiled at her over the rim of his coffee cup. "I notice you refer to the perpetrator as 'she.' Do you have anyone in particular in mind?"

"Dee," said Jenny.

Her response hit the room like a bombshell, creating ripples of tension. Peter made a choking sound and slammed his cup onto the table. McAvoy went rigid. The tendons in his fingers grew taut and the chalk squealed across the board and snapped in two. The longer piece fell soundlessly to the carpet, and he stared at the stub in his hand, as if he couldn't figure out how it had come to be there.

Peter was the first to recover. "That can't be, honey. Take my word for it. Dee's not a suspect."

"She is as far as I'm concerned. You'd think so, too, if you weren't blinded by her pot roast and her Swedish meatballs. And, oh, yes! Let us not forget her beef Wellington." Jenny tossed her head disdainfully. "Well, let me tell you something about Dee Chapin. She may be versatile as all get out and a virtuoso with a skillet, but outside the kitchen she's a—"

"Listen," said Peter, "it's obvious you don't like Dee, but that's no reason to accuse her of—"

"No *reason?* That letter arrived the day *she* showed up. And I'd like to know why you're defending her."

"I'm not defending her, honey. It's not a matter of taking sides. But the thing is—" Peter hesitated, ran a hand through his hair. "Dee's one of Gus's operatives."

"B-but I— You— It isn't—"

"It's true," said McAvoy. "Pete was stewin' about your safety, so I assigned Dee to keep an eye on you."

Jenny confronted Peter, her color high. "Why didn't you tell me?"

He lifted his chin and swallowed, as if his collar were too tight. "If I had, would you have let her hang around?"

"If you'd asked, I would have—if only because I can't seem to deny you anything! Why do you think I hired her in the first place? Because it obviously meant a lot to you, that's why. Heaven knows, it wasn't Dee's charm, and she's no great shakes as an operative. If she were any good at it, she'd be much more agreeable. Every time she opens her mouth, she puts her foot in it." Jenny swung around to challenge Gus McAvoy. "I'll bet I'm her first assignment."

"You got me there," he admitted. "She's been with me less than two months. She came highly recommended, though, and she's a whiz at writin' reports. Not that she's done this kind of work before, you understand, but she wanted to get some field experience under her belt, and this seemed like a good case for her to start with. She told me she could handle it and seemed real confident. In fact, at the time I thought she might be *too* confident, but I figured that was because her family's connected with law enforcement."

"That's funny," said Jenny, shaking her head. "She told me her family's involved in the arts. I wonder which is the truth."

McAvoy's eyes narrowed. His mouth hardened to a grim line. "Couldn't say, but you can be damn sure I'll find out." He wrote Dee's name beneath Bev Rudolph's, then glanced at Jenny over his shoulder. "Any other candidates?"

"Two," she said. "Toni Greer and Rita Eccles."

For Gus's benefit, Peter explained, "Eccles is Rudolph's roommate. The one with the sticky fingers."

"We also had a falling out," Jenny said. "The letter disappeared one afternoon, and I thought Rita had taken it, so I phoned her and asked where it was."

"Naturally she denied it." Before Jenny could ask Peter how he'd known, he said, "Dee brought the letter to me. She thought I should see it."

"You knew? You knew about it all along and you didn't let on?"

"Look, I realize it's no excuse, but I was hoping you'd take me into your confidence."

Jenny tried to look stern and couldn't quite manage it. The fact was, she should have told Peter about the letter, and he should have told her about Dee.

She attempted a smile, and that was more successful—especially when Peter smiled back. His hand found its way to her shoulder again, and this time she welcomed his touch.

"As long as we're baring our souls, are there any other secrets you'd care to share with me?"

"No, that about does it."

"Same here."

"Whew!" Peter wiped his forearm across his brow. "That's a relief."

McAvoy refilled his coffee mug, eyeing the chart he'd made on the chalkboard. "Any other suspects I should check out?"

"No one comes to mind," Jenny answered.

"So we have four women," said Peter, "all of whom fit the profile."

"Along with a dozen other people," McAvoy qualified. "Y'know I lifted quite a few prints from the scene. We might get a break there, if the perp wasn't wearing gloves, but that's a mighty big *if,* so I wouldn't count on it. And even if we're lucky enough to have some useful latents, I wouldn't hold my breath. I gave the prints I collected to a buddy who's with the Department of Justice. He'll run 'em through the computer as soon as he can, but it's gonna take at least a week to ten days. Even then, it's a long shot. DOJ's latent-prints system has a data base of six million but if our culprit's not a known felon, a state employee or in some other line of work that requires his prints be kept on file, a search'll give us zip, so we better hope we come up with some other leads."

McAvoy drew a question mark beneath the list of names, then underscored the center column. "What else can you tell me about the perp?"

"Nothing," said Jenny.

"It'd help if we knew why the perpetrator's doing this." said Peter.

Gus nodded agreement. "You said a mouthful, Pete. On one hand, we've got the possible assaults against Jenny. The brakes go out on her car, but they happen to fail in the driveway, so she's not hurt. The binding breaks on her skis, but since she's never skied before, she's on the beginner's hill. She gets off with a broken ankle, which is no small thing, but it's not enough for our perp. He—or maybe I should go with Jenny's instincts and say. *she*—wants more. But what is it she's after? What does she stand to gain? Why does she come at Jenny from a different angle? Is it just that Jenny's stuck indoors and not so accessible? Does something spook her, or does she deliberately back off? Is the next stage—the psychological attack—part of the plan? She writes the letter. She breaks into the apartment and wrecks the place. Where does that get her? Why does she take stuff like credit cards and college diplomas and leave other valuables behind?''

McAvoy paused for a sip of coffee. He turned his back on the chart, and looked from Jenny to Peter. ''The next step,'' he finished quietly, ''is to figure out the motive. When we figure out the 'why' of it, we'll have our perp.''

Friday again. Another wasted hour with the shrink. He was puffing on his pipe, as usual, and she, as usual, was listening to her internal clock, tuning out his silences and pretending to be attentive to his lectures.

The topic under discussion today was fire, which gave her a few uneasy minutes. She racked her brain, trying to recall an instance where she might have slipped up, made some casual comment that could have given her away.

That was the worst thing about lying. Keeping your stories straight. Remembering what you'd said, and when you'd said it, and who you'd said it to.

Everett might not be an Einstein, but he wasn't a slouch either. It took a lot of energy and plenty of smarts to keep him in the dark. She had to know when to talk and when to be quiet, when to smile and when to frown, when to be herself and when to slip back into character. And when she was in character she had to be on guard, constantly monitoring his reaction, trying to gauge whether he was convinced by her performance or if she ought to switch to a hard sell.

If she really needed psychotherapy, she'd never have been able to pull it off.

Sometimes she was amazed by her command of her role. But there were other times, like today, when she was in the midst of making the transition to a new part, and her authority was less complete.

How could it be otherwise when she was a mixture of three people? The woman she was, the personality she was playing, and the personality she planned to assume.

But forewarned is forearmed, so she'd come prepared. She'd even brought a prop to impress the doctor, courtesy of Jenny Spaulding, and when she'd walked into Everett's office, she'd held it so that he could easily read the title. Case Studies in Compulsive Behavior. *What a yawn.*

And did Everett notice? Not on your tintype! Not enough to detour his one-track mind. He'd picked up where they'd left off on Tuesday.

"Have you read the pamphlets on hypnosis?" he'd asked. "You have? Wonderful! Did they alleviate your fears? You're not sure? Well, what seems to be the problem? Loss of control? Concern that I'll take liberties and muck up your mind? Certainly, you're not worried about disclosing guilty secrets. Or are you?"

"I have nothing to hide," she'd assured him. "Even if I did, I wouldn't hesitate to share it with you. I know I'm protected by doctor-patient confidentiality."

"Good," he'd said. "Good." As if he didn't feel stymied, as if he hadn't lost round one.

She'd thought he was bluffing until round two began, and he'd said the magic word.

Fire.

He'd filled his pipe and held a match to the tobacco, puffed once or twice, then quite deliberately stopped. "You never talk about fire," he'd remarked, still holding the lighted match, "yet it has a special significance for you. Fire killed your best friend and her husband. When you wanted to get even with your former employer, fire was the weapon you chose."

The flame had burned down to the end of the matchstick. He blew it out, lighted another, and turned it this way and that, observing her closely, studying her trying not to stare at the flame.

The ploy was so transparent, she almost groaned. She could have predicted the next thing he said.

"Go ahead and look at it. I know how much you want to, only you're afraid it'll give you away. But when someone lights a match, perhaps it's natural to look. Perhaps you give yourself away by not looking."

Her response was as calculated as his staging of the scene. She had slanted brief, indifferent glances toward Everett, then the match, and said, "What in the world are you talking about?"

He didn't fall for her plea of ignorance. Not that she'd expected him to, and as the session wound to a close, he said, "You must realize this is a deep-seated problem. I can't release you from treatment until it's resolved. That's why I urge you to proceed with hypnosis."

He was like a dog with a bone; his persistence made her wonder how much he knew and how much was guesswork. And as she left the office, she thought, in at least one respect, Dr. Everett had hit the bull's-eye.

She did have a deep-seated problem. The doctor himself. He was a pain in the rump. And soon, very soon, she would have to eliminate him.

"WHAT DO YOU WEAR to a séance?"

Lila Darien stopped on her way out the door. "Whatever you'd wear to a farce," she said.

Jenny could hear her laughing all the way to the vestibule. An hour later, she asked Peter the same question. He responded with a question of his own.

"What's wrong with what you have on?"

"Nothing for an evening at home, but isn't a denim skirt a little casual for a séance?"

"I think you look nifty."

Jenny sighed. "You *always* say that."

"That's because you always look nifty to me." Shrugging, he added, "You don't take this business of communicating with the dead seriously, do you?"

Jenny didn't. Of course she didn't. If she had, she wouldn't be going to the séance. But others took it seriously, and she wanted to show respect for their beliefs. Besides, as she said to Peter, "What if we're wrong and Toni's right? What if there is something to it?"

The thought of attending the séance gave her the creeps. She couldn't shrug it off like Peter, or laugh it off like his mother, so she went into the bedroom and changed from her skirt and blouse to the purple coatdress Lila had picked up for her that afternoon. When she came out, Peter gave her a wolf whistle and told her she looked soigné.

She stuck out her tongue at him and went into the office to look up soigné in the dictionary; by the time she found it, it was eight-fifty-five.

They walked across the courtyard to Toni Greer's apartment, and when Toni ushered them into her living room, Jenny felt like a peacock.

Toni was wearing black. Bev Rudolph and Lurine Watley were wearing black. Two other guests whom

Jenny had never seen before were wearing black, and Peter was wearing his black crewneck sweater.

Toni invited them to be seated, then vanished through the swinging door to the kitchen without performing introductions.

Jenny sat on a sofa. Peter sat beside her. Beverly smiled and nodded, but nobody said anything, not even "hello." Jenny thought it must be the dirgelike music playing softly on the stereo that discouraged conversation.

"Not what I'd call an icebreaker," Peter whispered.

Jenny agreed. "I feel like I'm waiting for a bus," she whispered back. "Did you notice Toni's not wearing gloves tonight?"

"Yeah, I noticed, and I didn't see any scars."

Five minutes passed. Toni hadn't come back, and still nobody said anything. Jenny felt as if the others in the living room were staring at her purple dress.

"What are we waiting for?" Peter whispered.

"Another guest, I think." The answer came from Lurine, who was sitting opposite Peter. "That would make eight of us, including Toni, and she says even numbers are more enticing to spirits."

Peter nodded as if this made perfect sense. "Do you come to these things often?" he asked Lurine.

"As often as I can. They're deliciously bizarre."

"Should I have worn black?" Jenny murmured.

"No. Purple's an appropriate color."

"Soigné, too," Peter whispered.

Soigné or not, appropriate or not, Jenny felt out of place until the latecomer arrived and the séance got underway. With the dining-room lights turned off, and the only illumination provided by the single candle at the center of the table, the room was so dark, her purple dress looked black.

At Toni's request, the eight of them formed a circle with their hands flat on the tabletop, fingers spread, pinkies touching.

"Make yourselves comfortable," Toni said, and chairs creaked as everyone shifted about, complying with her directions. "Once we begin, do not break the circle, no matter what happens."

She gave each of them a cautioning look, then inhaled deeply, settled back in her own chair and trained her gaze upon the candle.

Quiet settled over the room, a silence so complete Jenny could hear a watch ticking. She glanced around the table, wondering whose it was, and then she caught a hint of movement from the corner of her eye and realized that Toni had gone limp and slumped over the table. Her head was bowed so that her hair curtained her face, and she was humming a song, a reverent, elegiac tune that climbed the scales until she was almost keening.

Something stirred in the darkness overhead, and Toni lapsed into silence. There was a faint rustling, as of taffeta, then the candle flickered and a breeze sighed past Jenny's cheek.

Toni stiffened and jerked upright in her chair, staring fixedly at the flame. "The veil is lifted. The spirit is with me. The spirit is within me. I am its vessel. We are one. Speak through me, spirit. Let me see the road before us and the road behind through your eyes, for there is one among us who is in peril. Let me speak with your voice, for there is one among us who needs counsel. Let me see with your wisdom, and I will not flinch. I will not turn away from the truth."

The candle flickered again in a swirling current of air. The rustling sound returned, grew louder, became a crackling, then swelled to a roar, and above the roar, a tormented wail.

"It hurts! Oh, God, it hurts! Please, make it stop hurting."

The breeze stopped, the sound receded, and the smell of smoke wafted over the table.

"There, there," Toni crooned. "Be not afraid. You are safe now."

Then, in a distant voice, like an echo, ". . . safe."

"The pain is gone."

". . . pain . . . gone."

"You are part of the infinite. Nothing can hurt you."

". . . nothing."

The candle flame leaped in a last breath of air, then steadied and brightened. The smell of smoke faded.

"What is your name, spirit?"

Silence. A whimper.

"If you would help us, spirit, tell us your name."

" . . . she called me friend . . . best friend . . . only friend . . . not true . . . none of it true . . . she hurt me . . . don't trust her . . . tell Jenny . . . mustn't trust her."

"Who, spirit? Can you tell us who?"

" . . . ssss . . . aaah . . . "

The candle flame flickered.

"Tell us her name, spirit."

" . . . ssss . . . aaah . . . "

"Sarah?"

" . . . ssss . . . aaah . . ."

"Stella? Sheilah? Sylvia?"

" . . . sseee . . . yaaah . . . "

"Her name begins with a *C*?"

" . . . tell Jenny . . . don't trust sseeelyaah . . . "

From the darkness came the scrape of a chair across the hardwood floor.

The circle was broken, and the candle flame flickered and died.

Chapter Fifteen

In the hours following the séance, several things became clear. Jenny didn't know anyone named Celia. She had never known anyone named Celia. After the events of the past week, she was in no mood to cope with Dee again, and she was in no mood to celebrate.

She would have called off the Superbowl party, if Peter hadn't advised against it.

"It'll give Gus a chance to look the suspects over and see what they're like firsthand."

"He won't learn much," Jenny argued. "Whoever's doing this is too clever to do anything that'll give her away."

"Probably you're right, but there's always a chance. And I promise you, honey, you won't be in any danger. I wouldn't ask you to go through with the party if I thought otherwise."

Peter reasoned with her in his best courthouse manner. He coaxed her with hugs and bribed her with kisses, and in the end she agreed to go ahead with the open house, with the provision that she didn't have to keep Dee on as her research assistant cum watchdog.

Peter said, "You've got a deal."

On Saturday morning, instead of canceling the open house, Peter paid a visit to Toni Greer and made arrangements to move the gathering to the building's recreation center.

When he got back, he told Jenny, "Mission accomplished. You won't have to worry about anything tomorrow but showing up."

And playing hostess to the woman who ransacked my apartment. "What about refreshments?" she asked.

"All we need is hot dogs, chips and dips, soft drinks and beer. Nothing fancy."

Peter apparently had thought of everything, but Jenny couldn't relax. She spent the rest of the day on pins and needles, hoping for the best, fearing the worst, and trying to comfort herself with the thought that perhaps no one would show up.

Everyone they'd invited came to the party, including Rita, who was the first to arrive, but as often happened when Jenny was prepared for disaster, the open house went smoothly.

The guests mixed and mingled and chatted and laughed. They danced and played cards and shot pool. They helped themselves to snacks from the buffet table. As game time approached, everyone gathered around the wide-screen TV for the kickoff, but only the die-hard sports fans watched till the end.

Peter was among them, and so was Dee.

She wasn't the only woman who chose to stay with the game, but she was far and away the most conspicuous about it. From the opening whistle to the final countdown, she stuck like a cocklebur to Peter's side.

There was, Jenny thought, an air of desperation about Dee. And when Rita asked whether she was upset that Dee was making a play for Peter, Jenny answered "no" without a moment's hesitation.

"What are you? Some kind of saint?"

"Look at her, Rita, and tell me why I should let Dee get to me. She's so obvious, it's pathetic. I almost feel sorry for her."

Jenny was well aware that Dee fancied herself an expert on many subjects. And having seen firsthand how versatile Dee was, she shouldn't have been surprised to discover that Dee was conversant with football. Yet Jenny was surprised by how well Dee spoke the lingo.

"It's like football's her first language," said Lurine.

"Girl missed her callin'," Raette agreed. "She should've been a sportscaster."

"Should've been one of the guys," Rita muttered.

Bev Rudolph responded with a supercilious *"Mee-aow,"* as if she were above such cattiness, but by half-time her own reaction to Dee was less than charitable.

Jenny listened with a growing sense of bemusement as Dee prattled on about conversions and safeties and laterals, about blitzes and shotguns and sacks. It became evident that she understood the system of downs. She knew the difference between play-action fakes and draw plays, between false starts and encroachments—

"She should've been a coach," said Raette. "She should be calling the plays."

"Calling 'em, hell! She's *making* them," said Beverly.

And Rita, incensed by Dee's flirting with Peter, declared, "If there's one thing I hate, it's a phony."

Now and again throughout the game, Gus McAvoy circulated about the room, taking orders for drinks. He blended into the crowd without becoming part of it. The professional observer, he kept his distance and at the same time contrived to hide his reason for being there behind a hearty exterior.

When the game was over, he was the last to leave.

"So," Jenny said as she wished him good-night, "did you learn anything from all this?"

McAvoy grinned at her, a twinkle in his eyes. "Dee knows football, but she doesn't know beans about Pete."

And that, Jenny realized, was a pretty fair recap of the afternoon. "What's going to happen to her, Gus?"

"I'll send out inquiries, and while I'm waitin' for replies I'll keep her busy shuffling paper."

"And then?"

"If it turns out she's our perp, God help her. I sure won't. Little lady's gonna find herself in deep trouble."

"What will you do if she's in the clear?"

The investigator shrugged. "I'll still have to fire her, because she hasn't been telling the truth."

OVER THE WEEKEND the wreckage in the apartment had been disposed of. The maintenance crew had come in Friday to change the locks, and to paint and hang wallpaper. Eventually Jenny would have to replace the big-ticket items that had been damaged beyond repair—her computer, for instance, and the living-room furniture—but the replacements could wait until she and Peter decided where they would live after they were married.

Less than two months remained till the wedding. Peter had offered to line up the church. Lila was working on her part of the guest list and making plans for the reception. Phyllis was collaborating with Lila and had taken charge of the invitations. Which left Jenny free to get back to work.

She had a book to write and only seven months till the manuscript was due. Her outline was gone, along with the majority of her notes, and for the time being at least she had no computer.

But these debits were offset by an endless supply of pencils and legal pads, and by her father's ancient Olivetti.

The typewriter was battered by its travels, but virtually indestructible, and the typeface was much more legible than her handwriting.

Her other assets included the knowledge she had acquired about the locale, the people and the events that were pivotal to Bradley Darien's story, and the collection of documents, correspondence, photographs and other memorabilia on loan from Lila.

She also had a series of tape recordings made by Bradley's family, by two of his colleagues and by several of his friends, which luckily for her had come through the break-in unscathed.

Jenny supposed the tapes hadn't been touched because they were labeled with the Darien name, but *why* they'd survived wasn't important. What mattered was that she had eight cassettes, each containing the recollections of an individual who had been close to Bradley Darien, each containing colorful tidbits of information, each highly personal, and each a gold mine to a biographer.

She'd recognized their value from the beginning, but she didn't give much thought to the ways she might use them until the morning after the Superbowl party, when it occurred to her that they captured a clearer picture of Peter's father than anything she could compose.

So why not go with the tapes as much as possible?

If she transcribed them, edited the narrative, weeded out redundancies and mixed in whatever facts were needed for clarification, would the book be too anecdotal? If it read like a tribute instead of a biography, was that necessarily bad? Would she be doing a disservice to history?

If she kept the narratives separate and identified her sources, a certain bias would be acceptable. Some sections would be more flattering than others, of course, but taken as a whole, the story would balance out.

Was there a better, more illustrative way to define Bradley Darien, than to portray him as others saw him?

Jenny didn't think so. And if it accomplished nothing else, taking this approach would enhance her sense of direction.

So she dug Gareth's well-traveled Olivetti out of the storage closet, slipped one of the tapes into Peter's Walkman and began the task of transferring Lila Darien's spoken words onto paper.

Even as she started, she realized it would be easier to postpone the job till she replaced her computer, but the structure of the book was suddenly so clear and so exciting that she didn't want to wait.

Besides, the manuscript for *Justice Denied,* the exposé her father had begun and she had finished, the book that had launched her writing career, had been typed on this same machine.

There was a certain appeal to that. A kind of continuum.

It gave Jenny a way of saying that, though Gareth Spaulding was dead, his traditions lived on in his daughter.

And since it seemed particularly fitting that she should write the last chapter of the Santa Marta trilogy on the Olivetti that had started it all, she pounded away at the keyboard, happily, for the rest of the day.

As well as the next.

And the next.

And the day after that.

Until finally, on Friday, the last tape was done.

Other things happened that week. On Tuesday evening, Lila phoned to say she had found the ideal consultant to help Jenny choose a wedding gown. She came by Wednesday morning with pictures of dresses and headpieces and swatches of fabric, and they were lovely, all of them. Really lovely.

But there was one special dress with butterfly sleeves and a bouffant skirt and a semicathedral train that was sheer magic.

Jenny was enchanted, much to Lila's delight. "That one's my choice, too," she admitted, holding up crossed fingers. "Now, if only your mother agrees. I faxed pictures of the dresses to her last night, so we should be hearing from her any time."

Phyllis called that afternoon to make it unanimous, but in the interim Jenny had second thoughts.

"This dress is so formal," she told Lila. "If I wear it, Peter will have to wear a tux."

"At the very least," Lila allowed. "A cutaway would be more appropriate."

"Either way he'd have to wear a tie—"

"Absolutely."

"And he loathes neckties."

"But he'd only have to wear one during the ceremony, and if he's not willing to make a slight accommodation, none of these dresses will work."

"I'm sure it won't come to that, but it's Peter's wedding, too. I think we ought to consult him."

"Very well, dear. If you insist."

Jenny did. She sought Peter's opinion that evening, and he laughed and said he'd wear a suit of armor if she wanted him to. "Whatever it takes to get you down that aisle," was the way he put it.

Jenny was touched by his reaction, and Lila was ecstatic. She made an appointment with the consultant for Jenny to come in for a fitting the following Tuesday, and fired off a fax to Phyllis, announcing all systems were go on the wedding gown and soliciting ideas for the attendants' dresses.

"Isn't that a bit premature?" Jenny asked. "Shouldn't the bridesmaids have some say in this?"

"Of course they should," Lila answered. "As soon as you get around to choosing them, I'd welcome their input, and I'm sure your mother will, too."

Jenny couldn't ignore such an obvious hint, and so on Wednesday night, while Lila and Phyllis kept the fax lines humming, she wrote letters to Betty Holtz and Juno Jasperwall, asking Betty to be her maid of honor and Juno to be a bridesmaid.

In a P.S., she confided, "For the moment both Lila and Phyllis are vying to become Mother of the Year. So far the three of us have seen eye to eye on everything, but I'm waiting for the other shoe to drop. You see, I've got a hunch they'll gang up on me if ever I disagree with them. So before you accept, I should warn you, if anything like this happens, I expect you to take my side."

The weekend brought a flood of mail. The guest list and samples of invitations from Phyllis. Pictures of wedding cakes and more swatches of material from Lila. A hurried note from Betty, the gist of which read,

"You know I wouldn't miss your wedding for the world. All you have to do is tell me when, where, and name the weapons. I'll be there with bells on, along with whatever garments Lila and Phyllis dictate."

In addition to this, there were brochures from photographers and caterers and florists, and a questionnaire from the local newspaper, soliciting details to be used in announcing their engagement.

Jenny read through it all, leaving the guest list till last. She pored over it, with Peter looking over her shoulder.

"Who are all these people?" she wondered.

"Beats me," he said. "I was about to ask you the same thing."

She sighed and met his gaze. "Do you ever get the feeling things are getting out of control?"

"If by 'things' you mean our mothers, yeah, I do."

"Do you think we should do something about it?"

"That's up to you, honey. Do you want me to have a talk with my mom, maybe head her off at the pass?"

"Not necessarily. Not if it doesn't bother you that she and Phyllis are . . . Well, I guess they're kind of taking over the wedding."

"Does it bother *you?*" Peter asked.

She shook her head. "They've been waiting for this for such a long time. But how about you?"

He smoothed a strand of hair from her cheek, the better to nuzzle her ear. "I have no objections, as long as they don't try to take over our honeymoon. . . ."

On Tuesday, as Peter was leaving for work, he invited Jenny to stop by the office when she was through at the bridal shop. "I'll take you to lunch," he said.

"It's a date," she replied.

She arrived at the offices of Darien and Darien at quarter past one, and ran into Gus McAvoy, who was on his way out.

"What's happening with Dee?" she inquired.

"Dunno. She moved out of her apartment the day after your open house. Nobody's heard from her since."

"She must've got wind we're on to her," said Jenny.

"Must have," said McAvoy. "But I do have some progress to report. My buddy at DOJ ran those prints for us, and we got a possible match on one of the latents. Turns out it belongs to a real bad apple, a repeat offender who did time as a juvenile for arson, felony assault and breaking-and-entering. Then, about five years ago, down in Tehachapi, she was indicted for murder, but before the authorities could bring her to trial, she skipped out."

"Who did she kill?"

"Couple name of Wyatt. He was her probation officer. Seems she gained their confidence, even lived with 'em for several months, and wound up slipping the wife a mickey and setting fire to their house."

"How awful!"

"Like I said, she's a real bad apple."

"And you found her fingerprints in my apartment?"

"I found a partial. Not enough for a positive ID. We don't have enough identifying marks to stand up in court, but personally I think little Celia's our perp."

Jenny paled. "Celia?"

"She's used several aliases, but she was born Celia Baumgarten."

"Did the computer give you her picture?"

McAvoy nodded. "For all the good it does. The Kern County sheriff says it's likely she's had extensive plastic surgery."

"So she didn't look familiar?"

"Nope, and all we know for sure is that she's a thirty-one-year-old Caucasian female, five feet five, slender build. No tattoos, moles or scars."

"That description probably fits twenty percent of the women in the state."

"And everyone on our list of suspects," said McAvoy.

ANOTHER PACKAGE WAS delivered that afternoon, shortly after Jenny got home. This one was from Brentano's, a bookstore she frequented. It seemed innocuous enough until she saw the title of the book inside. *Everything You Always Wanted to Know About Sports but Were Too Scared to Ask.* She stared at the subtitle, *A Football Widow's Survival Manual,* gripped by a feeling of déjà vu.

The book was the roses all over again!

Moving by rote, she made her way to the phone, dialed Brentano's, identified herself and asked to speak to the manager.

"This is he, Ms. Spaulding. How may I help you?"

"I received a book today—" At this point Jenny faltered, uncertain how to proceed.

"Yes?" the manager prompted as her silence lengthened. "Is there a problem with the order?"

"I—I'm not sure." Again she hesitated, her mind racing. If she said she hadn't ordered the book, that she'd never seen it before, hadn't even heard of it, the manager would think she was crazy. "I'm sorry to trouble you," she said at last, "but I wonder if you could refresh my memory. Things have been so hectic lately, I've forgotten whether I paid for the book or put it on my account." Forcing a laugh, she concluded, "To tell you the truth, I don't even remember ordering it."

"No trouble at all. I'm happy to be of assistance. If you'll hold on for a moment, I'll find the sales slip." The manager was gone before Jenny could reply, and in less than two minutes came back on the line. "Ms. Spaulding? According to our records, that order was placed by telephone just before closing Friday evening. The book was shipped the following morning, and per your instructions, the sales price, plus tax and shipping costs, were charged to your account. Your copy of the invoice should reflect the current balance."

She thanked the manager and hung up, debating what to do next. Should she call Peter at work and tell him what had happened, or wait till he got home? She was still trying to decide when the telephone rang.

"Miss Spaulding, this is Annette, the receptionist at Rapunzel's."

"Pardon me?"

"Rapunzel Salon. When you called last Friday, I overbooked Paolo. I wondered if we could reschedule your two o'clock appointment?"

Jenny was about to say, "There must be some mistake. I never heard of Rapunzel's," when it occurred to her that anyone could have phoned the salon and made an appointment in her name.

"When would you like me to come in?" she asked.

"We can still get you in tomorrow afternoon. Would three-thirty be convenient?"

"Three-thirty's fine," said Jenny.

The following morning Gus McAvoy staked out Rapunzel's. Jenny spent the day on tenterhooks, waiting to hear from the investigator and hoping her ordeal would soon be over. But at nine that evening, her hopes were shattered. McAvoy reported the salon was closed for the night, and the woman who'd made the appointment hadn't showed up.

Over the next few days, Jenny's worst fears were realized. It became increasingly apparent that someone was masquerading as her. Other articles she hadn't purchased were delivered. A gold-filled fountain pen arrived on Thursday, C.O.D. She returned it to the store. On Friday it was movie videos, on Saturday a seahorse for the aquarium, on Sunday a pizza, and Monday's mail brought a bill for concert tickets.

In each instance, Gus McAvoy checked with the sender and was told that the order had been placed by telephone.

Jenny felt a resurgence of hope the following Tuesday, when the manager of a restaurant she had never been to called to let her know he'd found the bracelet she'd lost while dining there the night before. But Gus's investigation yielded nothing useful.

"They serve cafeteria-style," he said. "You take a tray and dishes and go through the line. And busy? The place is a zoo."

"Do you have the bracelet?" Peter asked.

"Yeah, I got it." McAvoy fished a pearl-and-gold link bangle from his pocket and held it up for Peter and Jenny's inspection. "It's strictly fake, and not a good one. I figure it cost about two ninety-eight, tops."

"Can you trace it?"

"If I had a thousand men and unlimited funds, maybe. Even then it'd be a long shot." The investigator tossed the bracelet onto Peter's desk. "The manager said the owner didn't notice she'd lost it till she got home, and then she phoned.''

"So there's no way to tie it to anyone?"

McAvoy shook his head disgustedly. "None at all. But I've got my suspicions.''

Peter nudged the bracelet aside with the eraser end of a pencil. "I think we all do."

"Celia," said Jenny. "Aka Dee."

Both men nodded.

"I'd be careful who I trusted, though, till we get a positive ID," said McAvoy.

"How long will that take?"

"Hard to say. I sent a copy of the picture from Dee's personnel file down to Tehachapi, and I also showed it around the restaurant, but nobody recognized her—not that I thought they would, busy as they are. Anyway, I figure if she's Celia, she'd stick with what worked before and change her appearance."

"Any leads to her whereabouts?" Peter asked.

"Not yet. We followed up on her references, former employers, people like that, and got nowhere. None of 'em heard of Dee Chapin. It looks as if her employment application was one big snow job.''

"Have you spoken to her ex-husband?" Jenny inquired.

McAvoy did a double take. "Didn't know she had one."

"She told me she does. He's the reason she came to Sacramento."

Peter made note of this on a legal pad. "What else did she tell you about this guy?"

"Just that they met at UCLA and moved up here because he took a job as an accountant with the state."

"Did she say which department he was with?"

"If she did, I don't recall."

"Did she mention his name?"

"No, but it's possible Chapin's her married name. She talked as if she regretted the divorce, and I think maybe she still had hopes they might reconcile."

"Chapin, huh?" McAvoy paced back and forth in front of the windows, arms folded across his chest. "How many Chapins do you s'pose there are in Sacramento?"

"I don't know," said Peter. "But I think we'd better find out."

Chapter Sixteen

Less than two dozen Chapins were listed in the Sacramento telephone directory; however, none of them admitted to a connection with Dee.

There were, on the other hand, hundreds of state agencies, the majority of which could conceivably have accountants on staff. "We'll have to take Dee's picture to each office, run it by the department heads, and hope we get lucky," Gus said.

To ensure that they didn't overlook any agencies, they decided to visit them in alphabetical order. Gus suggested Jenny take *A* through *H*, Peter *I* through *P*, "...and I'll take the rest."

"Sounds good to me," Peter agreed, "except I'll handle any divisions of the Department of Justice, even if they fall outside my part of the alphabet."

"Gotcha," said Gus. "And I'll handle Department of Corrections stuff."

At eight o'clock Wednesday morning, Jenny started calling on the agencies she was assigned, beginning with the Department of Administration. She was somewhat dismayed to discover it was subdivided into bureaus ranging from the Administrative Law Office through

Finance, but all of them, fortunately, were at the same address.

Ten o'clock found her at the Department of Agriculture, and at noon she made her way to the Office of the Banking Commissioner. By the end of the business day she had worked her way up to Credit Unions, but as she told Peter and Gus, "No one recognized Dee."

The men hadn't learned anything either, so Thursday was more of the same, except that Jenny had decided to dispense with the crutches. She'd hobble into one department or another, find the accounting office and flash Dee's picture. The routine response was "Don't know her," "Never saw her before," or words to that effect.

By late afternoon, all she wanted was a hot bath and a place to prop her injured leg.

Friday dawned foggy and cold, and to break the monotony Jenny spent an unproductive hour showing Dee's photo around the Student Union at Sacramento State. From the campus, she drove to the building that housed the Energy Commission, and from there she went on to the Environmental Affairs Agency, then ended the day thumping through the maze of corridors at the Board of Equalization.

She had lost track of the date and didn't realize it was Valentine's Day until she arrived home and found a valentine from her mother in the mail. Thinking of Peter, she made a trip to the nearest shopping center, where she chose the most romantic card for him and a decidedly unromantic gift, but one she knew he would love—a pair of tickets to the next Sacramento Kings' home game.

That's the beauty of buying presents for a sports fan, Jenny thought. You can always find something he'll like.

While she was in the mall, the fog had grown appreciably thicker, and so had the traffic. It was bumper-to-bumper, stop-and-go in either direction on Fair Oaks Boulevard. By the time she turned onto the Parkway her already glum mood had gone into a steep decline, and if that wasn't enough, when she got back to the apartment she discovered another parcel had been delivered.

Her spirits hit bottom when she saw the package that had been left outside her front door.

There had been no unsolicited deliveries since Monday, no trace of the impostor since the call from the restaurant on Tuesday. After three hoax-free days, she had hoped the masquerade was over, but now she had proof that it wasn't.

Sighing with resignation, she unlocked the door and reached inside to turn on the lights, then slid the parcel across the threshold with the toe of her shoe and reluctantly followed it into the entryway, eyeing it all the while.

There was no return address on the wrapper, save that of the courier service, but from its size and shape, she guessed it was a box of candy.

She flicked on the living-room lights, and using the foot plate on her cast, skidded the package toward the telephone stand, where she sat down and debated whether or not she should open it.

She was still debating the pros and cons when the phone rang, and again she thought of Peter. Ordinarily he would have been home by now. Had he been detained by the fog and the traffic gridlock? Was he calling to let her know he was on his way?

She answered eagerly on the second ring, and an unfamiliar, faintly slurred voice replied.

"Miss Spaulding, this is Quinton Everett. *Dr.* Quinton Everett. I understand you and Peter Darien are engaged to be married—"

"Have we met?"

"Regrettably no, although I've heard a good deal about you from one of my patients." After an uneasy silence, Everett added, "I'm a psychiatrist," as if his specialty explained everything. But it didn't. As far as Jenny was concerned, it only deepened the enigma.

"Did your patient tell you Peter and I are engaged?"

"No. There was a special segment in the afternoon paper—"

"Of course," she murmured contritely. She'd been so busy playing detective, she'd forgotten the announcement was running today. "You were saying?"

"This may seem like an odd question, but I assure you I wouldn't ask it if I didn't feel it was necessary." Everett lapsed into silence, and Jenny waited for him to continue. At last he blurted out, "Is your hair light brown? Long? A bit wavy?"

Jenny pulled the receiver away from her ear, glared at it and unconsciously straightened her spine, preparing to do battle. "Listen, buster, I don't know what your game is, but—"

"This is no game, Miss Spaulding. You must understand, it's in your best interest to answer my question."

"That does it," she said. "I'm going to hang up."

"No, don't do that! If what I suspect is true, I've made the most tremendous mistake, and there's only one way to put it right."

"By harassing me?"

"Please, Miss Spaulding, I'm begging you. I need to speak to Mr. Darien regarding a matter of utmost importance. I wouldn't be troubling you, except that I've tried to reach him at his home and his office without success. I thought perhaps you might know where I can get hold of him."

Weird, she thought. *The man's definitely weird.* Had he been drinking? Heaven knew he sounded fuzzier and more hysterical by the minute. But it occurred to her he might be a client, and she reached for a pencil and notepad. "Give me your message. I'll pass it along."

"My dear young woman, there's no time for that. How can I convince you that every second counts? It's imperative that I see Mr. Darien tonight!"

"I believe you, Doctor, and I'll do what I can to help. If you'll tell me where you'd like Peter to meet you, I'll see that he's informed of your wishes."

"But that won't do! It's no help, at all! Apparently I haven't made myself clear—"

"That's my best offer. Take it or leave it."

Having no other recourse, Everett took it. He gave her the number of his private line, and an address on 25th Street, just off Capitol Avenue. "The street door's locked, but I've left the side door open. My office is on the third floor, and since the elevator stops running at seven, I'm afraid Mr. Darien will have to use the stairs."

With that declaration, the psychiatrist broke the connection, leaving Jenny to puzzle over their conversation.

Not that Everett's story had changed her opinion of him, but she was intrigued by some of the things he'd said . . . and somewhat alarmed.

She punched in the code for the cellular phone in the Maserati, wondering what alcoholic fantasy had prompted Everett to ask about her hair. Why had he insisted it was in her best interest to answer his questions? Did his ''matter of utmost importance'' have anything to do with her?

''Pete Darien here, stuck in the mother of all traffic jams.''

Jenny smiled, albeit shakily, but in the minute it took to relay Everett's message, she began to feel more confident. When Peter said he'd never heard of Quinton Everett, she replied, ''He's certainly heard of you. As a matter of fact, he seems to know quite a lot about both of us.''

''I take it you think I ought to go along with his request for a meeting?''

''Yes, and I think I should join you.''

''In this fog? You've got to be joking. Why would you want to go out on a mean night like this?''

''Maybe I'd like to satisfy my curiosity.''

Peter chuckled. ''Maybe you would at that, but if you wait till I get home, I'll satisfy the total woman.''

''Thank you, my darling. When this is over, I intend to hold you to that promise.''

''When what's over?''

''Our meeting with Everett,'' was her airy response. ''See you there.''

''Hey, Jenny! Not so fast. Can't we at least talk this over?''

But Jenny had had enough of talking for one day. Before Peter could get any further, she cradled the receiver and headed for the door, turning off lights as she went.

At the last moment, she hesitated, then went back to tear the wrapper off the unwanted parcel. As she'd suspected, it was a box of candy, and she took it with her when she left the apartment.

As long as she was going downstairs, she might as well get rid of it, and she could think of no better way to dispose of two pounds of chocolates than to leave them at Rita's door.

AS SHE PULLED OUT of the garage, Jenny switched on the car radio and tuned it to the station that ran traffic reports so that she could plot the fastest route downtown.

By the time she reached the end of the drive, she'd learned her choices were limited to slow and slower.

Visibility was so poor, an official with the highway patrol had issued an advisory urging anyone who didn't have to be on the streets to remain indoors.

There had been numerous minor accidents throughout the city, and one or two that were not so minor. An eighteen-wheeler had jackknifed on I-80, creating a bottleneck that closed all but one of the eastbound lanes, and there was an eight-car pileup on Highway 50.

But Jenny didn't have to monitor the news to know that the weather was bad. All she had to do was look through the windshield as she crept along the parkway.

With her shoulders hunched over the wheel she peered into the fog, and saw for herself that only pale, milky halos marked the spots where streets lamps burned. Trees, houses and other vehicles had simply vanished into the mist.

She took the Howe Avenue bridge across the river, then bypassed the freeway entrance, continuing on Howe until she came to Folsom Boulevard. After a right turn on Folsom, she had a fairly straight shot to Capitol Avenue. She turned the windshield wipers down a notch, leaned back in her seat and breathed a sigh of relief.

She was crossing 65th Street when a report on a two-alarm fire in the commercial district not far from Capitol Park caught her attention. With her gaze trained on the road, she felt for the radio controls, adjusted the volume and heard that emergency vehicles had blocked 25th Street between Capitol Avenue and L Street.

"Just where I'm going," she muttered. "Wouldn't you know it?"

Or as Phyllis was fond of saying, "It never rains but it pours."

From 30th Street, Jenny could see dull orange pillars of fire reflected by the foggy sky. According to the latest update, the blaze had been upgraded to three alarms and she decided to cut over a block on Alhambra Boulevard, take L Street to 26th and walk the rest of the way.

She could smell the smoke from the fire as she parked near Sutter's Fort, and once she was out of the car, the odor was strong enough to make her eyes water. Ash and oily particles of soot drizzled with the mist onto the sidewalk, making the concrete slippery underfoot. She turned up the collar of her raincoat, plunged her hands into the pockets and set off toward 25th.

She could hear a flurry of activity before she reached the corner—shouts, the sizzle of water rushing from the fire hoses, the roar of the flames. At the intersection, she could see the flotilla of emergency vehicles that filled the street and the fire itself, leaping from the windows of one of the stately Victorian mansions that had been converted to office suites.

Her orthopedist's office was on this block. In fact, the building that was on fire might be his.

Not only might be, Jenny realized as she stepped off the curb. It *was* his. She started across the intersection, mesmerized by the scene....

The car appeared out of nowhere.

She heard the purr of its engine and the muted swish of its tires against the fog-slicked pavement, and she knew disaster was hurtling toward her even before she saw the glow of headlights through the swirling mist.

She backpedaled to get out of the way, but the car swerved, and the headlights came closer.

She heard someone call her name, heard running footsteps and spotted a man racing toward her as she scrambled for safety. But her efforts to escape were too late. The car was moving too fast, aiming straight for her, and the curb was too far away. She'd never be able to reach it.

The headlights were almost on top of her when the man sprinted in front of them. She recognized Peter and froze. Even her heart seemed to stop beating.

Oh God, if anything happens to him, I don't want to go on living, she thought, and the next thing she knew, Peter had somehow wrapped strong arms about her waist and was dragging her toward the sidewalk. And then she was falling and so was he, and they were rolling toward the curb in a tangle of arms and legs, and the car sped by, so close she could feel the heat of its exhaust.

"Jenny! My God, Jenny! Are you okay?"

"Okay," she echoed weakly. "How 'bout you?"

"Fine," he answered, hoisting himself to his feet. "Damn, that was a close call! Are you sure you're not hurt?"

"Positive." She managed a ragged laugh. "I can't believe I'm still alive."

Clutching at Peter's hands, she stumbled to her feet and burrowed into his embrace. "If you hadn't been here—"

"But I was here! Thank God, I was here!"

"Did you see it, Peter? Did you see the car?"

"Yes, sweetheart. I didn't get a good look at it, but I'm sure it was a late-model Mercedes, either gray or beige."

"Did you see the license? It had a caduceus on it."

"So it's registered to a doctor.... What else did you notice?"

"Nothing. How could I? It happened so quickly. The car was just...all at once it was *there!* And I couldn't— No matter what I did, I couldn't— It was like the driver was deliberately trying to run me down."

"Shh, honey, don't think about it. Not now."

Peter trailed fervent kisses across her forehead, her temples, her cheeks. He found her lips and kissed them gently, almost reverently, and she kissed him back.

They moved to the sidewalk and stood there, clinging to each other, murmuring broken endearments, oblivious to their surroundings, until their heartbeats settled into a calmer rhythm and reality began to seep in.

Droplets of moisture had collected on Jenny's lashes. As she blinked them away, she became aware of the damp, biting cold, of a scrape on her palm, a bruise on Peter's cheek. She noticed the occasional car cruising by, the clouds of smoke drifting through the trees.

Observing that the fire seemed to be under control, Peter said, "I think you've had enough excitement for one night."

"I think we both have," she replied.

"Would you like to pick up your car in the morning and ride home with me?"

"We're not leaving yet, are we? What about the meeting with Dr. Everett?"

"He's dead, Jenny. He was dead by the time I got here." Peter frowned at the burning building. "I was talking to the fire marshal when you arrived. He believes the fire's the work of an arsonist. He said it started in one of the offices on the third floor."

Jenny moistened suddenly dry lips. "Everett's," she whispered. "Are you telling me he was murdered?"

"It'll take an autopsy to determine that, but it looks as if somebody—probably the same person who tried to run you down—didn't want him talking to me."

ON THE WAY HOME Peter put in a call to Detective Yeager, and reported the attempt on Jenny's life. He stopped to pick up some Chinese takeout, and when they got back to the apartment she set the table and transferred the food to what was left of her serving dishes, while he prowled from room to room, apparently lost in thought.

She called him to dinner, and when he saw the envelope with the valentine beside his plate, he gave her a befuddled look. "You didn't by any chance receive a package today, did you?"

She stared at him aghast. "Don't tell me the chocolates were from you!"

"Yeah, they were."

She buried her face in her hands. "If only I'd known."

Peter pushed away from the table. "You didn't look in the box?"

"No. I thought..."

"What did you do with it?"

"I gave it to Rita." The import of his question sank in and she lifted her head to inquire, "Was something else in there?"

"Your engagement ring."

She hurried after him as he strode toward the entry hall, and when he opened the door, they were greeted by a trio of well-wishers. Toni and Lurine caroled, "Surprise! When's the wedding?" and Rita offered a mock-disgruntled, "Took you long enough."

Their badinage seemed good-natured and cheerful, yet when Rita led the procession into the apartment, Jenny lagged behind.

Although Dee's disappearance was incriminating and she remained the most likely suspect, none of these women was in the clear, and looking at each of them, Jenny wondered, *Are you Celia Baumgarten?*

Is it you, Toni? Is that why you used the name at the séance?

Is it you, Rita? Are you Celia? Are you responsible for Dr. Everett's death?

Is it you, Lurine? Are you a murderer? Did you try to kill me earlier tonight?

And as she followed the others into the dining room, Jenny wondered whether there was any significance in Beverly's absence. Was she on duty tonight, or was she driving around the city in a late-model Mercedes with M.D. plates?

"I believe this belongs to you," Rita said. Grinning, she placed the candy box on the table.

"Yes, it does," said Jenny. "Thanks for returning it." She reached for the box, but Rita scooped it up.

"Don't I get a reward?"

"What do you have in mind?"

"I should say tens and twenties, but this is Valentine's Day and I'm a sucker for romance, so I'll tell you what I'm gonna do...." Rita angled a chair toward Jenny. "Sit here."

Peter groaned and clapped a hand to his forehead. "I think I know what's coming next."

"So do it," said Rita.

"Not yet," said Toni. "Wait till we set the scene."

She lighted candles and turned off the overhead lights, while Lurine found a sentimental ballad on the radio. Rita produced the jeweler's box that had been concealed in the bottom layer of candy and gave it to Peter.

"Whenever you're ready," she prompted.

While their uninvited guests looked on, he got down on one knee and took Jenny's left hand in both of his. "You know how much I love you—"

"You can do better than that," said Rita. "I want to hear you count the ways. Pretend you're arguing a case in front of a jury."

He shot her a reproving glance. "I can see you're going to be a tough audience."

Jenny put her free hand on top of his. "But I'm not."

"No, you're not," said Peter, "and you're the only one who matters, so I'll try to forget we've got witnesses and concentrate on you."

Even with the lights dimmed, Jenny was keenly aware that one of the witnesses might be her enemy, until Peter turned to her, his expression softening.

"I guess I haven't given much thought to why I love you. It's mostly something that I feel, and it's not easy to analyze or to put into words, but I can tell you the first thing that attracted me to you was your voice. Do you remember a year ago last June, you phoned the office?''

"And you answered," she said.

He nodded. "That was when I realized you have the sexiest voice I've ever heard."

"Thank you, sweetheart. I think you're sexy, too."

"My reaction was chauvinistic," he went on. "I'm not ashamed to admit it. I wanted to see if the rest of you lived up to your voice. The office was closed for the day, but I told you to come on up, and you did, and I wasn't disappointed because everything about you turned me on. Your hair, your eyes, the way you walk, the way you look at me. So I started out feeling like a stud, thinking maybe we'd have a little fun. But there was something in your smile that really moved me, so by the time we went to dinner you had me thinking of sweet music and dry champagne and feeling protective."

"That's why I felt so safe with you," Jenny replied softly.

"We were together that day...how long would you say? About two or three hours?"

"Yes, about that."

"Well, that was long enough for me to find out I wanted to see a lot more of you. And the more I saw you, the more I wanted to see. The more I learned about you, the more I wanted to learn, and by the end of two days I wanted to know everything about you, and by the end of two weeks I knew that would take a lifetime."

"But you weren't ready to make a commitment."

"No, and neither were you."

Jenny smiled into his eyes. "You were so open and honest, so generous. You seemed too good to be true. I was afraid of repeating my parents' mistake. Afraid to trust my own judgment. Afraid I'd lose my independence.''

"You weren't the only one, honey. And to top it off, I was scared to death the way we felt about each other couldn't last.''

"But it has. Not only that, it's gotten better.'' She placed her palm against his cheek. He was blushing a bit, and his skin was warm to the touch; her own face felt hot with color, but nothing could stop her from saying, "Every day I discover something new about you that makes me love you more.''

"Same here,'' Peter marveled. "I won't claim that I'll always understand you, but I know I'll always love you, and if you ask me why, I'd have to say it's because you're you. So, Jenny Spaulding, will you marry me?''

"You know I will.''

Her gaze never wavered from his as he slipped the engagement ring on her finger and sealed it in place with a kiss.

"Well done,'' Lurine cried, and the spell was broken. Toni burst into applause and Rita slapped Peter on the shoulder as he got to his feet. "Congratulations,'' she told him. "Now it's official.'' To Jenny she said, "You've got the guy, the emerald-cut diamond, and my very best wishes. Seems to me it's only fair that I should keep the candy. What do you think?''

"Rita, I'd say that's the least you deserve,'' Jenny agreed. Before her neighbors left, she made an excuse to take Toni aside and ask why she wore gloves.

Her cheeks pink with embarrassment, Toni confided, "I have a skin condition—contact dermatitis. It's nothing serious, but it can be unsightly.''

"I didn't mean to pry,'' Jenny replied. "It's just that Bev Rudolph said your hands were scarred.''

"Did she? I wonder why?"

"So do I," said Jenny.

"Well, I'm sure there must be a logical explanation. Maybe Bev knows how self-conscious I am."

"Yes," said Jenny. "That's probably it."

Chapter Seventeen

There was an article about the fire on the front page of Saturday's paper, but it didn't contain any new information. In an update on Monday, the medical examiner was quoted as saying the postmortem exam showed a high level of barbiturates in Quinton Everett's bloodstream.

"That's Celia's M.O.," said Peter. "In the Tehachapi murders, she put her victims out of commission, then set the fire that killed them."

"Gus gave me the impression she only drugged the wife," Jenny said.

"Maybe the husband was already asleep," Peter answered with a shrug. "After five years, what difference does it make? It's still the same M.O."

At Tuesday's appointment with the bridal consultant, Jenny discovered that her wedding gown was more beautiful than she had recalled, but she began to hyperventilate when she tried it on.

Eyeing herself in the mirror, she fretted about the train. "It seems to go on forever."

"Not to worry. You'll get used to it," the seamstress replied.

"What if I don't? What if I trip over it on my way down the aisle?"

"You won't, dear. Take my word for it. I've dressed many a bride, and I haven't had a casualty yet."

Till me, Jenny thought. She found it impossible to stand still for the fitting, and left the shop feeling like a pincushion.

That evening Peter told her the police had recovered Dr. Everett's car.

"I didn't know it was missing," she said.

"Well, it has been since Friday. Would you care to guess the make?"

"A gray Mercedes with a caduceus on the license plate."

"Right, except it was cream-colored."

"Was?"

"It's been totaled. They found it in a gully off Highway 50, near Placerville. Evidently, it went off the road on a curve, rolled and caught fire."

"Are they sure the fire wasn't set?"

"They seem to be, and with good reason. There was a woman's body in the wreck."

"Celia's?"

"They don't know yet. The body was badly burned. It's going to take a while to identify it."

On Wednesday, Jenny hit pay dirt at the Franchise Tax Board. She went directly from the state office building to share the information she'd unearthed with Peter and Gus.

"One of the auditors in the income-tax section recognized Dee's picture. Her ex-husband's name is Stanley Wyatt."

The men exchanged a startled look. "Figures," said Gus. "What d'ya wanna bet Stanley's related to the probation officer and Dee's on Celia Baumgarten's trail.''

"That would explain her lies to you. Her lies to Jenny."

"Too bad it doesn't explain where she is." McAvoy glanced at Jenny. "Did this auditor know whether Stanley's still in the area?"

"He said he'd seen him at a party just before Christmas." The investigator reached for the phone book as Jenny continued, "What puzzles me is why Dee wouldn't have gone to the police if she had a lead to Celia."

"Maybe she did," said Peter. "Suppose several years after the murders, she spotted a woman who looks like Celia. So she goes to the police, and it turns out the suspect fits Celia's general description. Same height, same weight and so forth. There's a strong resemblance, but there are differences too. Her hair color's changed, maybe the shape of her nose and her chin. Hell! With these new silicone injections, her whole face might be recontoured. And she's had time to establish a new identity. She has a different name, a different background and the documents to support it."

"I hear what you're saying. It would be her word against Dee's."

"Yes, and even if the police believe Dee's story, there are limits to what they can do. If they approach the suspect to question her, they've alerted her. The minute they're gone, she takes off. If they play it safe and take her into custody while they're developing a case against her, there's a chance any evidence they come up with will be ruled inadmissable in court. Which leaves them between a rock and a hard place."

"It's a no-win situation," McAvoy concluded. "No matter what the police do, they're screwed. The minute Celia gets wise to them, she pulls her vanishing act."

"Do you think Dee's been through something like this before?" Jenny inquired.

"Could be," said Peter. "It's obvious she's decided to get the goods on Celia herself."

Tangling with a cold-blooded killer, Jenny thought, would be a tricky enterprise. One that would require courage, steady nerves and boundless determination. One that would be challenging, fraught with danger and a bit foolhardy.

It was exactly the sort of thing she could imagine Dee doing.

THAT EVENING GUS PAID a call on Stanley Wyatt, and he confirmed some of their assumptions about Dee. "She claimed she'd seen Celia Baumgarten, but I never really believed her."

"Why was that?" McAvoy asked.

"Partly because of the timing. The first time she brought the subject up was a year ago, about the time our divorce became final, and I interpreted it as another attempt on Dee's part to monopolize my attention."

"She didn't want to end the marriage?"

"Hardly. She fought the separation tooth and nail, and when that didn't work, she trotted out Baumgarten. But she'd never met the woman. Neither of us had. I was living in L.A. when my brother and his wife were killed, and Dee was at Fresno State."

"You weren't married at the time of your brother's death?"

"No. We didn't even meet till—I guess it was about eighteen months afterward. That was when Dee transferred to UCLA."

"So how did she recognize Celia Baumgarten?"

"That's precisely what I asked, Mr. McAvoy."

"And what did Dee say?"

"That she'd followed the investigation of my brother's murder with a good deal of interest, and she'd seen Baumgarten's photograph in the newspaper and on TV."

McAvoy frowned. "That would've been four years before."

"Yes," said Wyatt. "You can see why I didn't put much credence in her claim. I'm sure I saw photographs, too, and I would've had as much interest in the case as Dee, but to be totally honest, I don't think I'd recognize Celia Baumgarten if I passed her on the street. And Dee admitted she'd changed. I remember she referred to Baumgarten as 'the chameleon.'"

"Yet Dee insisted she'd seen her?"

"It was more than insistence, Mr. McAvoy. She became obsessed with Celia Baumgarten."

"The way he emphasized *obsessed,*" Gus told Peter later, "kinda made me wonder whether Delores Chapin might be one of Baumgarten's aliases."

A week after the interview with Stanley Wyatt, Dee's whereabouts remained a mystery, as did the identity of the driver of Dr. Everett's car. But as February waned, there were no untoward incidents, and Jenny began to think that Gus's theory made sense.

Her cast came off on the last Friday of the month. That weekend she felt as if she were walking on air—except for an hour or so Saturday morning, when she had the final fitting of her wedding gown and anxiety welled up in her throat.

"I can't breathe," she gasped. "The bodice is too tight."

The seamstress whipped a brown paper bag out of her workbasket, and while Jenny breathed into the sack, kept up a line of soothing chatter. "The bodice is perfect. The whole dress is perfect, and you look perfect in it."

"And this bag makes the perfect accessory." Jenny inhaled gulps of carbon dioxide, studying her reflection in the three-way mirror. "Maybe I'll start a trend."

"Only if you carry a white one."

The seamstress worked at the zipper and the row of tiny buttons that fastened the back of the gown, and once Jenny was out of the dress her breathing problems cleared. She waited patiently while the seamstress wrote out the sales slip for the gown, the headpiece and the silk spool-heeled pumps, then completed arrangements to have the order delivered.

"If I may say so, I've never seen a prettier bride or a worse case of prewedding jitters. But it's a good sign, you know, for a bride to be nervous. It shows how deeply you care. And I predict you'll be calm and composed when you walk down the aisle and you and your groom will be blessed with the happiest of marriages."

Happy but short, Jenny thought as she got into her street clothes. I'll probably die of oxygen starvation before I leave the altar.

She wondered if Peter ever panicked at the thought of getting married.

MARCH ROARED IN like a lion, and a stream of wedding presents began pouring in. China and crystal, linens and flatware, salad bowls, crepe pans, egg timers, pasta makers.

Every day brought its quota of surprises.

A collector's edition of Emily Dickinson from Claude LeFevre. A mantel clock from Juno. A needlepoint footstool from Jim and Tina Bratten. A crocheted afghan, fine as a cobweb, from Betty.

By March 7, Jenny was on a first-name basis with the man who delivered for UPS.

She had to burn the candle at both ends to keep up with her regular work schedule and the other demands on her time. There were thank-you notes to write, parties to attend, phone calls from her mother, phone calls from Lila, a spate of details for the wedding and reception to see to.

In the midst of all this, it became obvious that she and Peter were running out of space, so she began preparations to sublet her apartment and move to his condo.

On Friday the thirteenth, her neighbors in the building surprised her with a lingerie shower, and their gifts rounded out her trousseau.

Phyllis was due in on Saturday, the fourteenth. To make room for her, Peter would be staying at his place. That night was their last together until the wedding, and Jenny hoped to make it memorable. She modeled the shower gifts for him, and when the fashion show was over Peter showed his appreciation by kissing her as if he were memorizing the taste of her skin, by touching her as if he never wanted to stop and holding her as if he would never let her go.

When Jenny woke up the following morning, his arm was a sweet burden about her waist, his head was next to hers on the pillow and his face was the first thing she saw. She lay still, not wanting to disturb him, counting the hours till March 21.

Starting tonight, they'd be separated. Six days. And six nights!

How could she bear going to bed without him? Sleeping without him? Waking to find him gone?

He hadn't left, and she already missed him.

And she realized she couldn't wait till they were married.

A few hours later Phyllis arrived, catatonic from fear of flying, but by evening she had unbent enough to charm Peter's Uncle Max at a family dinner.

On Monday Jenny took Phyllis on a tour of the city. Lila came along, and while the older women saw the sights of old Sacramento, Jenny did some shopping.

She bought gifts for her attendants: a white jade pendant for Juno, amethyst for Betty. She bought a music box for Lila, a porcelain figurine of a Spanish dancer for her mother, a leather desk set for Peter, a white lace mantilla for herself.

Her arms were full by the time she bought wrapping paper and ribbon, and she was taking her purchases back to her car when she suddenly had the feeling she was being followed.

She spun around, looking back the way she had come, and saw nothing out of the ordinary, but the feeling persisted as she hurried on to the parking ramp, and it recurred from time to time for the rest of the day.

While the three of them were having lunch, during a visit to Crocker Art Gallery, while they were touring the Capitol she sensed that someone was watching her, observing her slightest move, waiting to pounce.

She tried to convince herself she had nothing to worry about, tried to blame the feeling on an overactive imagination, but that night she couldn't sleep. Hours after Phyllis had gone to bed she paced from room to room, from window to window, her ears attuned to the smallest sounds, her eyes scanning the darkness, fruitlessly searching for the source of her fear.

The sky to the east began to brighten, and still wide-awake, she watched for the morning, gripped by the kind of foreboding that would have prompted Toni Greer to say, "Somebody just walked over my grave."

TUESDAY PASSED IN a blur of weariness, Wednesday in a blur of activity as out-of-town wedding guests flew in.

Jenny made three trips to the airport that day. On the third, she picked up Juno Jasperwall and Claude Le-Fevre and drove them to their hotel.

Juno and Claude were fellow New Yorkers. They were writer and editor, as well as confidants who often behaved like Punch and Judy. Their friendship was characterized by constant bickering, and that afternoon was no exception.

They were bickering when they came down the concourse. They were bickering as they jockeyed for position in the baggage-claim area. They were standing by the carousel, waiting for their luggage, before either of them took any notice of Jenny.

Claude said, "You needn't have done this—"

"But I'm awfully glad you did," said Juno.

Claude shoved his glasses higher on the bridge of his nose. "You know, Juno, I wish you wouldn't take it upon yourself to finish my sentences for me. It's—"

"Maddening?"

"I was about to say annoying. It's an awful habit. Makes you sound like—"

"A smart aleck."

With that, the editor snatched up his briefcase and his canvas weekender and marched toward the exit. Juno signaled for a skycap's assistance with her bags, linked arms with Jenny and followed at a leisurely pace. As the revolving door deposited the three of them outside the terminal, she remarked, "You're looking wonderful, all starry-eyed and in love."

Jenny managed a shaky, "Thanks," and dissolved into tears.

Juno was horrified and Claude solicitous. "What did she say to upset you?"

"N-nothing," Jenny answered. "I seem to cry at the drop of a hat these days."

Which was true, she acknowledged, as she brought the car around. If a salesclerk said, "Have a nice day," she responded with tears. If Lila asked whether she preferred tea or coffee, more tears. If Phyllis told her she had a phone call, on went the waterworks. And if anyone made a personal comment, she wept inconsolably.

Phyllis didn't know quite what to make of her hypersensitivity, but Lila seemed to think it was a normal reaction. "When you're about to be married, it's natural for your emotions to be close to the surface."

Jenny wasn't sure what to believe, although she knew it didn't help that she felt desperately lonely without Peter. But the separation was almost over. They'd be married in another three days. Actually less than that. Only sixty-eight hours. And with Betty arriving for the rehearsal this evening, and the dinner party afterward, and notes to write and packing to finish, the time should go quickly.

She would get through it somehow, and so would her tear ducts.

PETER'S BACHELOR PARTY was slated for Thursday night. Late that afternoon Juno declared, "It's always been my contention, if the groom's entitled to a night on the town, the bride should have one as well."

Lila, Phyllis and Betty thought this was an excellent idea. Jenny agreed in principle, but after she'd yawned her way through dinner, the other women could see that what she really needed was a good night's sleep, so when she suggested they go on without her, no one argued.

"Don't wait up for me," Phyllis said as they left the restaurant.

Jenny assured her she wouldn't.

She was home by eight-thirty, in bed by nine, asleep as soon as her head touched the pillow, and when some small sound woke her, her first thought was that she must be dreaming.

Her bedroom was dark. She knew it couldn't possibly be morning, much less *Saturday* morning, yet she could swear she'd heard...

There it was again! Out in the living room. Someone was humming the "Wedding March."

Phyllis?

No, the night was still young. It was only nine-forty-five. Phyllis wouldn't be back for hours.

But if it wasn't Phyllis—

Her eyes opened wide. She was instantly alert, staring at the flickering streamer of light from the hall, listening to the scrape of a match, an odd hissing noise, the soft voice humming, moving toward the entryway, growing slightly more distant, finally stopping.

She became aware of other sounds. A footstep? The squeaky hinge on the door to the medicine cabinet in the powder room?

Then the humming resumed and Jenny threw back the covers. She slipped out of bed and made her way quietly to the hall. Once there, the chill draft that curled about her ankles told her the door to the balcony must be open, and when she stepped to the center of the hall she could see the writhing shadows cast by the half dozen candles that were scattered about the living room.

Beyond the candles, out of her line of sight, she caught a hint of brighter light.

Drawn by the music, she started along the hall. She felt more bewildered than frightened until she advanced to the point where the powder room came into view, and she saw the wraithlike figure of a woman standing before the mirror.

White. Dazzling white. She had never seen so much white.

And then the humming stopped, the woman turned and Jenny froze.

It's my wedding dress. She's wearing my wedding dress. And the headpiece!

Concern for the garments set her in motion, propelled her into the living room, restored her voice. "What do you think you're doing?"

"What I'm best at," came the answer in an amused, vaguely familiar voice.

Again Jenny hesitated, studying the woman. She tried to make out her features, but the veil reflected the brilliant light of the powder room, obscuring her face.

"Do I know you?"

"Not as well as I know you."

"But we've met."

"Tsk, tsk. Does it bother you that you can't place me? Shall I jog your memory?" The woman laughed. "Hi-dee-ho. How's every little thing goin'?"

"Raette?"

"Ta-dum!" She dipped a curtsy.

"How did you get in?"

"That question's unworthy of you, Jenny. I'm in and out of Toni's office six days a week."

"So you have a key. That doesn't give you the right to use it. What are you doing here? And why are you wearing my dress?"

"Because it suits me. As to the purpose of my visit, I should think it would be obvious."

"But it isn't."

"How tiresome. I guess I'll have to explain. Raette's the character I've been playing, and I don't mind telling you she's not one of my favorites. It isn't terribly exciting, being a gullible yokel, but I was stuck with the part."

"Stuck with it? I don't understand."

"Really? I thought by now you'd have found out about Raette and Wyatt . . . and Celia."

The name caused a rush of adrenaline. Jenny took a step toward the phone—

"I wouldn't." Celia issued the command in a menacing tone, and as she spoke she displayed the equally menacing revolver, which was cradled in her left hand. "Now, where was I? Oh, yes. I was telling you about Raette. You know, boring as she was, all I wanted was to take her place."

Keep her talking, Jenny thought. *Stall for time. Try to catch her off guard. Wait for the opportunity to make a break for it.* "You didn't intend to kill Raette?"

"Only physically. I've kept her personality alive, and God knows I've used it to greater advantage than she ever did. But I didn't intend to kill Wyatt." Celia glanced toward the medicine cabinet, but even while she admired herself in the mirror, she kept the barrel of the gun trained upon Jenny. "I've never been able to figure out why he tried to rescue her."

"She was his wife. He must've loved her."

"No. He might have loved the idea of being a hero, but he couldn't have loved Raette."

"Why not? The way you played her I found her very likeable."

"Most people did, but you must admit she didn't have much to recommend her. She wasn't pretty. She wasn't smart. About the best thing you could say for her was that she was wholesome. And eager to please."

Celia turned away from the mirror, and walked out of the pool of light. Jenny watched with horrified fascination as she sauntered across the shadowy living room. The long satin train missed one candle... two...

"Please, be careful of the dress."

Celia paused to gather up the train. "Men like that, don't they?" She continued on to the makeup case she'd left on top of the stereo and let the folds of satin fall. "Well, don't they?"

Jenny knitted her brows. If only she weren't so cold, she might be able to think clearly. She might be able to devise a means of escape. "I'm sorry, I—"

"We're never going to get anywhere if you don't pay attention." Celia brandished the gun as casually as if she were wagging a finger, then set the weapon down within easy reach. "I just made the observation that men like women who are eager to please. Do you agree?"

"Some do, I suppose."

"Does Peter?"

The question sent Jenny's mind into a tailspin. "Is he... Is that why..."

"He's been my goal all along. You're nothing more than an obstacle."

"And Dr. Everett?"

"Another obstacle."

"What about Dee?"

"A nuisance. She'd been on my tail for months, but I didn't know why. I assumed she was a spy for a man I used to work for till I came to your Superbowl party. The way she stuck to Peter made the penny drop. It was like she was trying to protect him or something, and it occurred to me she might not be who I thought she was, so when I left here that night, I led her to my place and got the drop on her. She spent the next two weeks in an abandoned refrigerator car down at the freight yards."

"S-so she's dead?"

"After her adventures with the railroad and Everett's Mercedes? What do you think?"

Jenny hugged her arms to her sides. She couldn't stop shivering.

"The light dawns," Celia proclaimed. "I must say, it's about time." She opened the makeup case and withdrew a can of charcoal-igniter fluid, which she set on the stereo cabinet, and a vial of capsules. "If there's one drawback to the kind of acting I do, it's that I rarely have an audience." She tilted her head to one side, contemplating the label on the pill bottle. "No. That's not true. I usually have an audience, but my audience doesn't know I'm performing, so no one appreciates my artistry."

Do something, Jenny told herself. *Say something! At least you can go down fighting.* She lifted her chin, notched her hands on her hips. "You expect your victims to stand up and cheer? Isn't that rather like murdering your parents, then throwing yourself on the mercy of the court because you're an orphan?''

"*Brava,* Jenny. It's gratifying to see that you can rise to the occasion.''

"It's better than sinking to your level.''

In retaliation for this comment, Celia hurled the pill bottle at Jenny. She made no attempt to catch it, and held her breath as the vial clattered to the floor. Celia maintained the illusion of calm, but as she picked up the can of igniter fluid, thumbed open the cap and proceeded to splash the liquid around, every movement expressed a fury that might soon spin out of control.

"Suit yourself," she muttered, squirting igniter fluid over the stereo cabinet, the bookcase, the carpet. She squirted the drapes, and the breeze carried a fine spray back toward her. "It's no skin off my nose either way. But if I were you, I'd take a capsule and go to sleep. No muss, no fuss, no pain.''

Jenny's hands tightened into fists. "What makes you think, with me out of the way, Peter will settle for you?''

"What makes you think he won't? Would you like a preview of coming attractions?'' Without waiting for a reply, she pulled off the veil, the headpiece.

"You'll tear them,'' Jenny cautioned. "They're very delicate.'' And then she noticed Celia's hair, and words seemed to catch in her throat.

"I'd say it's a pretty good match, wouldn't you? Isn't it amazing what a good eye for color and a little bit of dye can do?''

Jenny stared at the spill of glossy sherry brown hair that was incredibly like her own, hoping to find some difference in shading...in texture...in style....

"Of course I will confess I needed a sample to get the color exactly right."

"From my hairbrush," Jenny whispered, despairing.

She might have given up and retreated to the bedroom, if Celia hadn't been after Peter.

If Celia hadn't become overconfident.

If she hadn't smiled.

If she hadn't trod on the veil and headpiece.

If she hadn't dragged that glorious satin train through puddles of charcoal-igniter fluid as she saturated the lamp shades, the tables and chairs.

If she hadn't been working her way toward the dining room, where the wedding presents were stored.

"You know, Jenny, sometimes you have to play the cards you're dealt. It's not too late to take those capsules. I wish you'd think it over."

Instead of retreating, Jenny advanced. "You're the one who should think it over. Once I'm dead, you can't hurt me any more, but you'll be alive, and if you so much as look at Peter you'll see hatred in his eyes. You'll see contempt. You'll see disgust. You'll see revulsion. He will never—absolutely *never!*—fall for a cheap phony like you."

There was a moment of utter silence, then Celia let out an outraged howl and made a dash for the gun, but before she could reach it Jenny rushed her. The speed of the attack took Celia by surprise; the force of it threw her off balance against the sliding screen door. She dropped the can of igniter fluid and tried to push Jenny off, but no matter how she fought, Jenny would not let go. The screen sagged beneath them, and then it gave way and Celia tumbled onto the balcony, while Jenny broke free.

She grabbed the handle of the patio door and attempted to close it, but the satin train of the wedding gown was protruding into the room, and she knew that she wouldn't be able to lock the door with all that material blocking the track. She bunched up the fabric and was shoving it outside, when Celia started to scream.

Jenny looked up and saw that one of the drapery panels as well as yards of white satin had knotted about Celia. She was flailing about, in a frenzy to unwind the fabric. Staggering to her feet, she screamed louder than ever, and some of the neighbors across the courtyard came to their windows.

Jenny dragged the drapery panel off the rod and threw it onto the balcony. She slammed the door, locked it and went for the revolver, only to halt, midstride, as Celia's screams rose to a crescendo.

Turning, Jenny saw tongues of flame leaping along the drapery panel and the cathedral train—lapping at oatmeal linen, consuming white satin and lace, racing toward Celia, threatening to engulf her.

"She's on fire," someone shouted.

"Call 911."

"Trip the alarm."

Jenny ran to the kitchen for the fire extinguisher, but she couldn't find it. Not in the pantry, not in the cupboard beneath the sink, not in her catchall drawer. And then she remembered the fire extinguisher had been damaged in the break-in.

She ran back through the dining room and out the front door to get the extinguisher from the corridor, but by the time she got back the screams had stopped and the balcony was deserted. Smoldering strips of satin hung from the railing.

Numb with shock, Jenny opened the door and stepped onto the balcony.

In the courtyard below, the neighbors were gathered around Celia's body.

Epilogue

After the nightmare came the dream.

It wouldn't have been possible without Phyllis and Lila.

On Friday, while Jenny was making her statement to the police, her mother and Peter's scoured the city to find her the perfect wedding gown.

It wouldn't have been possible without the seamstress, who worked overtime to make the necessary alterations.

The new gown was fashioned of watered silk. It had a princess bodice detailed with seed pearls, Juliet sleeves and a full, graceful skirt with only a hint of a train. Jenny liked it better than the dress she had chosen. It didn't overpower her. She felt comfortable in it.

On Saturday, when she and her attendants gathered in the dressing room at the church, the seamstress commented on her composure. Lila and Phyllis were nervous. Betty was tense. Juno was on edge. But Jenny remained calm even when it dawned on the others, somewhat belatedly, that they hadn't thought to replace her veil.

But Jenny had.

She'd brought the white lace mantilla and a mother-of-pearl comb, and everyone agreed they were the ideal complements to the gown.

A steady flow of guests arrived. The chapel was full. As the time for the ceremony approached, one of the groomsmen ushered Lila to her pew. While Phyllis waited for her escort, she and Jenny had a few minutes alone. Phyllis admitted she had butterflies in her stomach. Jenny said she had butterflies too, although she didn't.

She had planned on walking down the aisle by herself, but at the last moment she asked her mother to accompany her. "I know it goes against tradition, but I'd really appreciate it if you'd say yes."

This had never been part of Jenny's dream, but it suddenly seemed appropriate. And when she stood beside Peter at the altar and the minister asked, "Who gives this woman in marriage?" Phyllis answered proudly, "I do." She embraced Peter, then turned to embrace her daughter.

"I love you, Mom," Jenny whispered, and Phyllis whispered back, "Your father would be very proud of you." Both of them were misty-eyed as she placed Jenny's hand in Peter's, and before she moved away she broke with tradition again. "Take care of each other," she said quietly, so that only they could hear. "The two of you are very precious to me."

Everyone agreed that the ceremony was beautiful, and what made it especially beautiful was that the bride and groom were so obviously in love.

During the reception, which was held at Max Darien's house, the newlyweds observed all the rituals. They greeted their guests, talked with friends and acquaintances, posed for photographs, ate the wedding supper, drank champagne toasts and led the dancing. But they had eyes only for each other.

They cut the cake. Jenny threw her bouquet, and laughed when Rita caught it. Still laughing, Jenny went upstairs to change to her going-away outfit. She said quiet farewells to the seamstress, to Juno and Betty, to Lila and Phyllis. She told each of them, "I can't thank you enough." And then it was time to leave.

Juno asked, "Where are you going on your honeymoon?"

Jenny smiled and said, "I've no idea." All Peter had told her was to pack for two weeks of warm weather and sunshine.

When she came back downstairs, Peter was waiting, and the orchestra was playing "As time Goes By."

He held out his hand. "How about one more dance?"

"Love to."

He took her out to the terrace, where the evening was fragrant with spring, and they held each other and danced in the moonlight. Now and again they kissed.

"Where are we going on our honeymoon?" she asked.

"Does it matter?"

"Not as long as we're together."

He led her through a series of spins, and their movements were perfectly synchronized. "This has been a great day," he said. "On a scale of ten, I'd give it a twenty."

She rubbed her cheek against his, sighed with contentment. "It's been the best day of my life."

Peter folded her closer. She felt his mouth curve into a grin. "It's not over yet, Mrs. Darien. This is just the beginning."

Mrs. Darien... That's me! Jenny thought.

And her cup of happiness overflowed.

HARLEQUIN

I N T R I G U E ®

A SPAULDING AND DARIEN MYSTERY

Now that you've read the heart-stopping conclusion to the
Spaulding and Darien mystery series, be sure you've read the
books that started it all. Join this engaging pair of amateur
sleuths—writer Jenny Spaulding and lawyer Peter Darien—on
all their cases:

#147 BUTTON, BUTTON: When Jenny and Peter first met,
they had nothing in common—except a hunch that Jenny's
father's death was not a suicide. But would they live long
enough to prove it was murder?

#159 DOUBLE DARE: Jenny and Peter solve the
disappearance of a popular TV sitcom star, unraveling the
tangled web of Tinseltown's intrigues.

#171 ALL FALL DOWN: In an isolated storm-besieged inn, the
guests are being murdered one by one. Jenny and Peter must
find the killer before they become the next victims.

HARLEQUIN®

I N T R I G U E®

INTRIGUE IS CELEBRATING ITS 200TH BOOK!

Remember all those great adventures you had....

The SHADOW OF THE MOON spills across the stained carpet and the NIGHTWIND howls. You're stuck in a HAUNTED HOUSE in which HIDDEN SERPENTS slither. There's a CALL AFTER MIDNIGHT. It's THE LATE GENTLEMAN ringing to see if that FACE IN THE MIRROR is SUITABLE FOR FRAMING. "What do you mean?" you scream wildly into the phone. But the only reply is WHISPERS IN THE NIGHT.

And the suspense continues! Don't miss Intrigue #200
BREACH OF FAITH
by Aimée Thurlo

Two hundred escapes into suspense and danger with mysterious men brave enough to stop your heart.

IF TRUTH BE KNOWN, a trip through a Harlequin Intrigue can be STRANGER THAN FICTION!